À mes parents. À Mr. Getz.

The Walls of Flemington

JULIETTE ROGASIK

ISBN: 1493625969
ISBN-13: 978-1493625963

Printed in the US by Amazon
www.amazon.com

CONTENTS

"Here the sons and daughters of Abyssinia lived only to know the soft vicissitudes of pleasure and repose, attended by all that were skilful to delight, and gratified with whatever the senses can enjoy. They wandered in gardens of fragrance, and slept in the fortresses of security. Every art was practiced to make them pleased with their own condition. The sages who instructed them told them of nothing but the miseries of public life, and described all beyond the mountains as regions of calamity, where discord was always raging, and where man preyed upon man."

~ Samuel Johnson, *Rasselas*

1 THE BOY AND THE CRICKET

The doorbell rang once and woke her, and made her gasp. It was quiet, so utterly quiet. Behind the shadowy curtains large flakes of snow invaded the dark sky that reached across the plains and fell behind the Rocky Mountains—one with the night, one with the silence. She sat up and reached for her glasses on the small wooden tabletop at her side. Who is it that rings?

She stepped warily out of bed. The floor was cold under her bare feet. The kitchen door stood partially open, a warm glow seeping into the dim hallway from within. The domestic stepped from the light and walked towards her, attentive and alert.

"Miss?" it said.

"What time is it, Alon?" she asked.

The domestic looked pale in the obscurity. "It's 3:42 AM. Should I answer the door, Miss?"

She looked towards the front door. Whoever stood behind it had not rung twice, and there was a deep silence inside the house. "Who is out there?"

"It's a child, miss."

"A child? What on Earth—" She stared once more at

the door, vaguely distinguishable in the darkness against the furthermost wall, and then back at her domestic. "A child? At this hour?"

"Do you wish me to answer the door?"

"Turn on the lights," she said, "I will get the door." As she walked, she tucked her hands in her elbows and pressed her crossed arms against her nightgown. The chilly air, hanging motionless around her, made her shiver. She grabbed a silk shawl from the wooden coat rack below the staircase and wrapped it around her neck. The domestic followed her. She opened the door without a word.

Standing pale and quiet, his feet buried in the thin snow that rested on the doorstep, was a boy. He seemed no more than ten years old. He stared up at her patiently. His placid blue eyes seemed to glisten in the warm light that fell onto the elusive features of his face from behind the open door.

The boy said something in another language, and she did not understand. His voice was small and frail, yet composed.

The woman stared at the shadowy figure bundled in layers of snow-covered clothing, the whitish forehead and auburn curls tucked under a large fur hat. The child wore black aviator trousers and a well-tailored merino duffle coat.

She stood in the light of the entrance and her lips were parted slightly as though she were about to speak, but whatever words she wanted to say she could not find, and for a while she said nothing. The child's eyes did not wonder from hers, even when briefly she turned her gaze towards the solidary night and the waves of snow that twirled in the silence.

He waited patiently. He held something in his hands—a small black cricket—cupped in both palms like a treasure. It did not move. It did not chirp. Maybe the cold had killed it, and maybe the boy had not realized.

"*Domina*, may I have a horse?" he said, with the same pale voice as light as an echo, an echo that the night had lifted with snowy arms and carried to her ears.

"Please, *domina*, will you give me a horse?"

2 HENRY

It was early in the morning—Mr. and Mrs. Rhynes were still asleep. Henry's eyelids opened, but stabbed by the white light seeping through the window and onto the floor of the room, they snapped shut again. His limbs were numb. He had been sleeping in one position for too long. He made a grumbling sound at the bottom of his throat, as if calling his body back to consciousness, and then some muscles in his face twitched, as if to chase away a fly that has alighted there.

He reached his legs in front of him, sliding them along the cold floor. It felt good to stretch them. Again, the eyelids fluttered open, hesitantly, slowly. His heavy head was still resting on the wooden planks; he looked around with an unsteady gaze.

He had fallen asleep at the foot of Etienne's bed, and he could hear the boy snore. American music flowed from an old CD player on a low shelf near the bed. It was barely audible. The album lay next to it. There was a large slant across the transparent casing, and tiny dust particles had settled on the broken surface, forming a thin white sheet. A few words composing the old album title had been handwritten long ago on the glassy plastic with a black permanent marker. An arm hung down the side of the bed, motionless, pale from the coldness in the room, its fingers so relaxed that they seemed to melt down into the floor, although they barely touched it. Getting clumsily up, Henry rushed out of the room.

He had always liked the silence that reined over the rooftops as daylight rose slowly from its serene sleep. The lighthearted chirping of birds would slowly tear through the silent wind that rushed between the trees. The breeze would slither across the green pastures and pour into the tranquil ponds, carrying in its invisible arms the scent of fresh grass and flowers moistened by dew. He had always taken pleasure in the sounds and smells of the morning. They filled his carefree little heart with joy. Henry had no conception of time, but he always knew morning was here when the first light of the day caressed the roof of the house. When it did, he would push the front door wide open and rush outside. He would dash across the field and around the village houses, his eyes fixed—full of wonder—on everything that would cross his path. It was his moment of tranquility and freedom.

The front door was locked and Henry whined, disheartened. The brisk walk down the hallway from Etienne's room to the entrance had shaken away the drowsiness from his body, and he stood on his hind legs, pressing his paws against the wood. He touched the glass frame with his nose, and the warm vapor of his breaths condensed into fine droplets on the cold glass and blocked his view. He dropped his legs back down. His claws, softly touching the floor as he paced nervously to and fro along the door, made the sound of tiny little beads on a stone surface. He sat back on his haunches, whining quietly. And then for a while, the soft and pure silence that had settled in the house during the night came back again, disturbed solely by the even sound of Henry's breathing. He scratched at the door quietly, then yelped once—twice— and growled, but the door did not budge at his cries.

"Hush, Henry!" a voice whispered from a second room down the small hallway. It was a woman's voice. At her call, Henry stopped his yelping and flopped his fluffy body onto the cold parquet floor. He ran his paws along the slit in the entrance, between the floor and door. The breeze flowed like a soft liquid between his claws. Through the window resting near the door, not so far above him, he could see the branches of the trees reaching upwards. Their many leaves were pale green and healthy, and the wind hissed through them.

And still further above, far, far above the trees, he could see the Lights, the many round orbs of artificial luminance aligned across the great Ceiling, separating the colony from the dark immensity beyond. The Ceiling and the Walls locked them all away from the dangers of the cosmos, from the great void, from the ocean of emptiness that cradles the universe in its arms.

3 DREAMS

"Follow me, Adelene," Olio whispered through the muffled sounds of machinery and the hum of air rushing through ventilation shafts that reverberated in the long steel passageway. BioLED lights stretched along the low arched ceiling. Their pallid glow diffused on Olio's slender composite body as he motioned the young girl to follow. The broad white doors opening onto the Universal Library of the Twenty-Ninth Division had long since vanished behind her, along with the endless hustle and the voices that echoed vaguely behind the polished walls of the immense edifice. In the dark corridor, all was muted, silent.

At times it frightened Adelene to think that she had spent all her years in *The Inceptum-Fidelis*, navigating through the dark, eerie vastness of Space towards the New World that still lay more than thirteen light-years away. Those whose parents had decided to remain on Earth lived in eternal freedom, not trapped in the entrails of a gigantic steel monster. She had always dreamed of seeing with her own eyes the blue-green planet that her parents had left seventeen years ago. She had seen planets before—when the ship drifted close to one, the entire Colony would gather in the Observatoriums and watch in awe the ethereal spectacle—but these were lifeless, hostile gas giants and uninhabitable wastelands of molten metallic rock. She yearned for the lush, oceanic paradise teeming with life that her ancestors called home. Now, its sun was lost among the multifarious stars in the universe, nearly two light-years behind them.

"Olio, please tell me where you're taking me!" Adelene said, unease forcing her voice down to a whisper. "I didn't shelter you from the Police so you'd take me on little errands through restricted areas! You've said it yourself: there are microbots everywhere in these parts of the ship, filming everything. The Authorities will see us and we'll get arrested! Take me back!"

Olio grabbed her hand. His touch was reassuring. "I just need to show you something. Come!"

Adelene could hear her own footsteps echoing far into the semi-darkness as she followed the lean figure further down the irregular passageway.

***

The passage ended abruptly on several round doors built close together along the vaulted walls. So far from the center of the Division there were no lights, and Olio began to project from his eyes a beam of bluish light that illuminated his view. Barely pausing to examine each of the doors, Olio turned towards one of them. He pressed his body against its cold, hard surface, and seemed to be listening for something behind the door. The whirr of working mechanisms and the faint drone of translucent radiation shielding sounded from behind. This was the right door.

"What's in there?" Adelene asked, panting as she watched Olio manipulate the door's coded access key under the glow of his lit eyes, "What are you doing? How do you know the code? Don't tell me you've been here more than once!"

Olio said nothing. The heavy door let out an odd beeping noise, and opened slowly. Cautiously, the two figures entered the vast room beyond. They were met by a blast of cool air. As the door shut behind them, the basal hum of mechanical ventilation ceased, locked out behind it. Adelene shivered in the sudden, eerie chill. She took the android's hand as her eyes wondered across the unfamiliar room.

"Ow! Stop squeezing me so hard, you're hurting!" cried Olio, breaking the spectral silence. The door had shut behind them.

"Where are we?" The girl's words were barely audible, as if she had asked the question without truly expecting an answer.

In front of them, in perfect alignment, lay a multitude of large white spacecrafts along the cold flooring that extended far off on the right of the circular door. The cockpit of each vessel seemed quite spacious, yet the room was too dark for Adelene to see through the wide windowpane at its front. Pairs of wings stretched out of the spacecrafts' sides. They reminded her of the strange wings of planes, the like of which had once been displayed as a hologram at the P.M.E. She had never truly understood how such ridged wings could carry people in the air.

"You threw away your contacts, right?" Olio asked, fretfully scanning her eyes.

"Yes, I *did*," she answered peevishly. "But can you stop doing that!"

"Doing what?"

"Scanning my face with that laser thing in your eyes. Myrna does the same thing and it bothers me. Now can you tell me where we are?"

Once more her words met no response.

"What's behind that wall?" she asked Olio, staying close to him. The furthermost extremity of the room was not a wall, but rather a massive, vertical steel door that seemed to lock out behind it something ominous and hostile.

"Space," Olio answered, "These are emergency escape vessels. They can travel back to Earth. Look, I modified this one a bit." He rushed cheerfully towards one of the spacecrafts. "It's an Alcubierre Ship now. I replaced the antimatter compartment with Exotic Matter of negative mass-energy, so that the vessel itself can manipulate planet-scale quantities of energy, create a distortion in space, and reach its destination at superluminal speeds without shredding the laws of Einsteinian physics. It's called the Alcubierre drive. This ship can go faster than light, Adelene! I made it for you, so you can go back to Earth!"

The girl smiled. "You did all of this for *me*?" She looked up at the great spacecraft in awe, moved by Olio's words.

The android stared proudly at his creation. "This is what you've always wanted, isn't it?" he said.

There was a pause, so intense in the darkness that it seemed to last hours, and then Adelene signed. "You don't understand. Everything I told you about this—all of it since the beginning—it was all just... *dreams.*"

Olio had never understood the concept of dreams. *Dreams are things human beings have when they sleep*, Adelene had once explained, *They are images and thoughts that go on in our heads. They make no sense and they're crazy.* Still, dreams remained a hazy, mysterious idea to him. He knew that sleep, this strange automatic deactivation at night, was one of the many concepts whose secrets were reserved to living creatures—and he soon lost interest in it. *Sometimes people have dreams even when they're awake*, Adelene would tell him, *and we have foolish thoughts that follow us everywhere. But no one should have dreams. They're Cursed. We don't need dreams to live.*

We have to be happy the way we are.

Olio could see Adelene's pale hands shaking. There were tears in her eyes now, and they glistened in the blue light beaming out from Olio's visage and weakly reflecting off the spacecraft.

"There's a difference between dream and *reality*, Olio. I know it's hard for you to understand this, but you have to. I can't leave the ship. No one can leave the ship; that's the Law and you know it. You have to take me back home, and we must never talk about this ever again." The last few words left her mouth on a quavering voice—a voice of fear, a voice with its own expression, on the verge of terror.

And Olio saw this. He saw this in her eyes, and in her trembling hands, and in those last few words. Showing no regret, no resentment or disappointment, he obeyed. Nonetheless the enthusiasm he had felt not long before had left him, and it was in silence that he gave one last look at his Alcubierre ship, and that the two of them traced their steps back to the door.

Olio touched his palm to the door. He looked uncertain.

"What's wrong?" Adelene asked. The spectral coldness in that dark metallic cave was as stagnant as the murky waters of a pond, and it enveloped her like an invisible shroud. "Please! Open the door and lead me out of this place!"

His robotic eyes avoided hers. "It has never closed behind me before. I've always made sure to leave it open." He scanned the door with the blue beam of light still projecting sharply from his face, and mumbled something, half to himself.

"What did you say?" Adelene's heart pounded in her chest, so hard she could almost hear it.

"There's an key-in section, but I don't know if the code's the same on this side."

Adelene shivered. "Just try it. Go on. Try the other

code."

Olio paused, and then she heard him mutter quietly again in that strange mechanized tone as he agilely entered the code.

They stepped away from the door in silence, and waited. The door did not budge.

"*Key incorrect.*" The voice came from the door itself. "*Key incorrect.*" It was a clear, feminine voice, eerily calm. There was another sound too, an acute ring so low it was almost inaudible to Adelene. And yet next to her, Olio squeezed his hands firmly upon his ears, pained by the noise. Finally there came a jumble of distinct beeping sounds so strange it seemed the door's interior mechanism was shutting down altogether, and then there was silence again.

"What do we do now?" Adelene whispered, her voice tense and uneasy. Both stood very still.

"I don't know," Olio answered. His arm was stretched across her chest protectively, as if to shield her from the door. And then he heard—both of them heard—the sonorous sound of the alarm, the one that was never, ever supposed to ring. It seemed to come from everywhere at once; a deep, atonal buzzing that ricocheted across the strong metallic walls. Its deafening sound rose to their ears so suddenly that simultaneously the android and the girl froze, flashes of blinding red light accompanying the noise and plunging them into utmost confusion.

"Olio!" Adelene screamed, "Olio, we're caught!"

A flash of light and Olio's silhouette appeared next to her, and then again vacant darkness, and the echo of the alarm. Another flash, and it was the door she saw, barely discernible, firmly shut and ominous. Then once more it was shadows. There was no way out.

4 HEARTS OF LEAD

The classrooms at Middleton School were all old-fashioned, with high glass windows and wooden floorings. From most windows one could see the gardens where the smaller children played at noontime, and a few houses neatly aligned along the gravel roads. The trees looked healthy and green. The rays of light seeping through the windows lightened the green hue of the vine leaves as they made their way up the old stone walls year by year.

The window by Adelene's desk was partially open, and the cool spring air stroked her hair. Her cheek rested on the palm of her hand. She flicked a fly off her desk and watched it stumble away out the window and disappear, a tiny black pixel adrift in a world of colors. Sometimes she felt like that too—tiny and insignificant, a speck floating through the Universe.

The girl next to her nudged her. "Pay attention, Adelene."

"I am paying attention."

"You're not." The girl laughed quietly. "I'm going to have to give you a copy of my notes again, aren't I?" Her name was Eugenia Robinson. She was a scrawny red-haired girl with a sunny countenance and freckles all over her face. Like Adelene, and most other kids at the school and all the other schools in all thirty divisions, she had lived all her life on the ship. No one younger than eighteen had ever seen the Earth. *We're so lucky*, Eugenia had said to her once after a history class, *Imagine how it is on Earth. War, disease, hunger, poverty. It must be horrible to live there. Imagine having no one to care for you? No one to give you nice clothes or even to cook your food. Here we have everything we could possibly want. It makes me feel guilty sometimes!* And she had laughed gawkily in the folds of the finely woven silk scarf around her neck.

The Teacher paced back and forth between the rows of seats, and for a second its bright robotic eyes fell onto Adelene. She felt a cold shiver creep through her. She had never liked looking into a Teacher's eyes. They were too cold, too mechanical, too unhuman.

"Miss Adelene," the Teacher said, "Please advise your classmate to pay attention while the course is in session."

Eugenia looked up with a snubbed air. "If I may defend myself, Teacher, this was in fact what I myself was telling Adelene to do as you heard me speak."

The Teacher turned its back to them. "I also plead you, Miss Adelene, to advise Miss Eugenia to know her place, and to keep her mouth shut when she has not been given permission to speak."

Eugenia opened her mouth to speak but said nothing. Instead her cheeks turned red and she buried her face in her notes again to conceal her irritation.

The class resumed it course. The Teacher's voice droned in Adelene's mind like the voices a boring television show. The diagram of the Inceptum Fidelis on the screen at the front of the room floated into her mind like an image in a dream. She had heard this lesson a thousand times before, over the years, each year slightly more detailed than in the previous year. The structure of the ship was simply fundamental and mandatory knowledge that each inhabitant of the Middle Generation had to learn. "As you all know, the Southern Wheel is composed of fifteen Divisions, each a kilometer long, nine hundred meters wide and seventy-five meters high, connected to one another at a 'northern' and a 'southern' point. The Northern Wheel is likewise composed of fifteen Divisions, including our own, the Twenty-Sixth. As you see here, both Wheels are connected to the horizontal axis that stretches twenty-five kilometers between the positron reservoir of the antimatter engine, which propels the ship forward at 30,000 kilometers per second, and the water reservoir installed in the great beryllium shield at the frontal extremity.

"Now, the gravitational pull that you feel right now, as you sit in your chairs, is created by the rapid spinning of our Wheel. This centrifugal force gives the impression of gravity exactly as it is on Earth, and can be calculated using the equation..." The soft robotic voice seemed to mingle with the sound of the ventilator as Adelene dozed off again.

On her desk were faded little hearts drawn with a lead pencil. It was Emmeline's lead pencil. Emmeline had four of them, Adelene remembered, and this had been her desk. The pencils were long, wooden writing utensils with a grey tip of lead that had to be manually sharpened every once in a while with a special object. Adelene had seen a few artists use them before, but Emmeline was the only one who used them at school. She would write her notes on paper made of cellulose fibers.

Using paper is killing trees, some kids would say to her when she first brought her notebook to school in Sixth Grade. *No, they don't kill trees on Earth anymore,* Emmeline would reply, *this paper was synthesized at a lab my grandmother worked at.* Then some bad-mouths would retort, *That's not true. Earth is an immoral place—full of lies and greedy people. They*

15

don't care about trees. Emmeline never knew what to answer. She had never known her grandmother but in pictures. She would try to hold back tears that glistened in her emerald green eyes. *Leave her alone!* Adelene had said to them one day, *None of you know what you're talking about—And how would you like it if someone talked to you like that?*

Ever since that day, Emmeline and Adelene had been great friends. But Emmeline had not been back in a year. She had never told anyone where she had gone, not even Adelene. Some said she had moved away, perhaps to the Southern Wheel, but there were whispers that she'd been Detained. *I think the Onweald is hiding things from us,* some had said slyly, crowded around a detached lunch table, *Emmeline was probably caught and Detained for sedition—or worse, taken as one of the Onweald's wives.* Adelene never believed the whispers. *That's nonsense,* she had blurted out, *My father worked for the Onweald, and I met His Excellency once. He's a respectable and admirable man who genuinely cares about us. He would never do anything like that.*

Emmeline was a slight girl, sweet and quiet. She had a pretty disposition and never bothered anyone, and the worse offense she'd ever committed was drawing hearts on her desk. She was barely fourteen when she disappeared.

The bell rang. It was an old bell sound, like the one at the Church, except shorter and drearier. Outside, the Gardeners trimmed the bushes and the sprinklers shot out graceful jets of cool water, spinning around in little circles and dressing the soft green grass in beady little droplets that glimmered softly under the Lights.

5 NOISE

It all happened again and again and again, so that time seemed to stand still, and the past seemed to have vanished.

More hostile blaring from the alarm.

More flashes of red light.

Adelene grabbed Olio's smooth, cold arm. In the confusion they heard the clamor of robotic voices rising above them, from nowhere and yet from everywhere. "Confidentiality breach," the voices said, in droning unison, "Unauthorized Intrusion Alert. Section 911482, Emergency Escape Vessel Containment. Escorted Female Human detected at –0.94 meters from Entrance X."

All the commotion—the noises, the lights—all of it was aimed at hunting them down. "They found us! Olio, get us out of here," she cried, her eyes darting in all directions.

"I can't; we're trapped! I'm so sorry, Adelene. This is all my fault! I'm so sorry!"

He pulled himself away from her. Through the flashes she saw his dazed expression, his panic. And she felt hers, too, deep inside, the tightness in her lungs. It was a chocking feeling. The sinister walls enveloped her, imprisoned her in the cold darkness.

"This is all a dream," Adelene heard herself murmur, "Soon, I'll wake up, and all of this will disappear… It is all just a dream."

Darkness.

Light and noise.

Darkness again. It had become an unceasing pattern.

"You stand in Violation of the Law." The monotonous robotic voices echoed above them again. "Under the Orders of The Onweald, you must remain where you are and abandon any further Unlawful Stratagem. Surrender to His Excellency, All-Powerful and All-Controlling."

"Break the door!" Adelene suddenly screamed, "Break it, now!" Her voice trembled. Her eyes were wide with fear.

Olio's eyes fixed themselves incredulously onto hers. "What did you just say?"

"You're strong enough to break through that door, Olio! It's made of metal, break through it!"

"I can't! You know we must obey!" His voice was so similar to those sounding above them, that Adelene could scarcely tell them apart in the confusion, and it frightened her. But there was—there would always be—something peculiar to Olio's voice, something almost human.

The voices far above were lifeless, echoing noises. Remain where you are and abandon any further Unlawful Stratagem.

"Just do it!" Adelene cried out to Olio again. Fear was coiled around her body like a snake, and she struggled to free herself from it. "Olio, pretend this is all just a dream!" She grabbed his arm again, and twisted him towards her. "Do you hear me, Olio? Remember what I told you about dreams? The crazy ideas? Well now this is your dream, and you will disobey. Break through that door and get us out!"

They had all been Programmed to Obey. A robot was a machine—a supernaturally strong, unarmed machine that never questioned or declined orders. A robot followed voice commands, and motion commands. Perhaps, in rare cases, it could reach a semi-sentient intelligence level and appear to think for itself. It could see the difference between a machine and a living being at an emotional level, and perhaps become self-aware and understand its own purpose. But never yet had a robot disobeyed the Authorities.

There was a sudden explosion, a great bolt of sound through the darkness, through the flashes and the unceasing blare of the alarm. The robot had crashed through the entrance, dragging behind him the frail young girl. The metallic voices bawled and shrieked from above in panic, and finally the spectral shadows of numerous droids formed across the high ceiling—dark, agitated forms. They had entered the vessel containment armed and alert, through the many pipes slithering along its walls. It was from them that the voices came, and they gave garbled orders all at once, louder and louder, circulating in the air across the semi-darkness, confused and disoriented. A cloud of black smoke rose slowly from the damaged entrance. A droid aimed and shot in its direction, and so followed the others, until the detonations of their laser missiles engulfed all other sounds.

Finally the shooting ceased and the droids scanned the vaulted door. The two fugitives had vanished. There was silence. The deafening alarm and the flashes—all of it—had ceased.

Target out of range, the lifeless voices droned, Follow through. And the droids floated out into the dimly lit passageway.

6 SARA

Chestnut trees leaned upon a broad, earthy path. The path staggered past the trees, its blunt, edgeless cobblestones jutting out of the earth, upturned, here and there, by heavy roots thrusting their tangled spines out from underneath. And then, further down, it ran along the fencing of the grazing land, quite far from the evening lights of the thick-clustered houses aligned along the bustling streets of the town. It sunk behind the soccer field, into the small woods beyond. From behind the trees there stretched the East Wall, vast, rigid, cold. It grasped the colors of the Sky, the beautiful Earth Sky that no child in this world had ever laid eyes upon, and it made believe that it was there—It made believe that the Earth Sky was there for all to look upon. And yet it was only the Ceiling, and the Walls. And they locked out the stars.

Ever since the Construction, ever since the Great Departure, in all the many days and months and years that followed, no human hand had ever touched the Wall. No one had ever touched its ridged surface, except Sara.

She was six years old, and there were tears in her heart. Her tiny hands had felt the Wall's smooth white texture, the cold stillness of it, forever marking the border of the world she knew. Maybe the tears had come out after all, for her cheeks felt warm and wet, and her breath was short. Maybe it was just the snow, the many flakes falling and swirling onto her from above in the shrill wintry air, melting with the warmth of her body. Strands of blond hair stuck to the girl's humid face. A cold chill ran through her, a sudden choking feeling, as if she had been plunged into an immense darkness.

There were no Walls on Earth, her mother had once told her, *Just the Sky, and the Mountains.* There had been sadness in her mother's voice that day—deep inside—a quiet sadness. Sara wondered how the world would be without the Walls, and without the Ceiling. She tried to imagine the Mountains. And then she heard the Nurse approaching behind her, climbing slowly up the snowy hill and calling to her, a dark shadow in the clouds of falling snow. She felt the Nurse's slender fingers wrap around her wrist and gently pull her away from the Wall. She blinked away the tiny snowflakes resting on the tips of her dark eyelashes, but did not look up at the Nurse's serene robotic eyes.

"There, there, dear child," the Nurse's placid voice rang in the girl's ears, "This is no place for a little girl. Is it tears you shed here? You mustn't cry, my love." Carefully, as she spoke, the Nurse wiped away the salty tears from Sara's cheerless hazel eyes. Her hands were very smooth. The voice was soothing.

"Is it true, Nurse?" Sara asked, her voice small and frail.

"Come. We must go back, little one. You will catch illness." The Nurse's grip on her wrist was strong. It hurt to resist.

"Is it true?" Sara repeated, "Is it true what that lady said? I will never see the Far Away World?"

"This *is* the World, my child," the Nurse answered, lifting the girl delicately into her arms to shield her from the cold.

Not many remembered the day they were told. For most, the memory eased itself out, slowly floating away, burying itself deeper and deeper as time went by—as the months and years went by. A child was born into the world and saw it as it was, simply seeing, and discovering. Life was the humid smell of autumn leaves, the warmth of the Lights, the taste of snow. Life was the velvety softness of stuffed animals, the soothing voice that sang the lullabies at night. And then life became language. The child asked the questions, and the adults gave the answers. The child was told about the ship, and then the destination—the mysterious New World—far away. Then the child was told about death, and that he was part of it. He was part of it because it was part of life, like the taste of snow. It was hard to understand death. It was hard to accept death. It was frightening, and it gave him nightmares. And yet somehow, maybe by instinct, he knew that it was there, revolving around him. The leaves in the trees died in the fall, and the fish died in the ponds. Then at night it was the Lights that died. But the day that he was told the truth about the world, the day he learned that for him—and all the others born with him—there was no New World awaiting, he shed tears, and they made a scar in his heart.

7 FLEMINGTON

Adelene stumbled out into the streets of the Division, her breaths short, her heart throbbing in her chest— rhythmic like the sound of the alarm, dizzy from the piercing screech of the missiles—pounding, pounding, echoing in her head like the droning robotic voices. The tiny steel door closed itself behind her and locked out the nightmarish passageways, the suffocating darkness, the shadows. For a moment she stopped, letting her eyes adjust to the warm brightness of the streetlights.

She had lost Olio. They had been separated somewhere in the entrails of the ship, frightened and confused, surrounded by the electric buzzing of old ceiling lights, the hum of the ventilation shafts swirling in the cold air that slithered endlessly through the passageways. Olio had burst through a heavy framework of metal beams stretched along the flooring and swiftly but carefully had led her down that opening into vaporous darkness. "Straight down, Adelene," he had called to her through the unearthly haze, "Continue straight down until you reach an exit. Don't look back." The light beams from his eyes had fallen upon her, gleaming against the yellow steam rising from the lungs of the ship. His words had come like an echo to her ears, mingled with other echoes—the voices—the hostile, deathly voices of the Authorities. She had listened to him without a word, and she could not tell how long he had remained with her from then on. Soon there had been no sound but that of her own footsteps and of the puffing, growling mechanism resonating through the vaulted walls, closing in on her, clawing at her back in that ethereal darkness. Then suddenly the passage had ended, closed off by the small door that, at her approach, had sunk down like a heavy blade into the floor in front of her. It had opened onto the Twenty-Ninth Division.

The Twenty-Ninth was a large town—a busy town. Flemington was its name, like the great artist. From the warm days of summer to the biting chill of winter, its Main Square bustled with androids, personal vehicles, men and women in fancy clothes. There stood the largest theatre, the finest restaurants, the greatest museums and galleries, and all the gossip of the world, slipping in the narrow streets from one fluttering voice to the keen ear of another. The stately entrance to the Universal Library had been built along the West Wall, and filled, each year, with waves of eager gentry from faraway Divisions. It was a town of entertainment and pleasure, romance and art, health and diversity, ruse and secrecy, and whispers.

Whispers. That night it was whispers.

Adelene came out from the darkness onto a dusty sidewalk. There was a rush of fresh air. It wrapped itself softly around her neck and caressed her hair. She stood where the narrow street ended, sliced by the West Wall. It was from the Wall itself that she had emerged, from that forbidden passage into the dismal depths of the Ship—of the World. The thought sent shivers up her spine.

She was alone.

Leaves rustled in the trees daintily aligned along the

sidewalks. Between the low buildings, the shadows of men and women stretched, shrunk, danced along the smooth white walls like flames, and from one window opened silently onto the night air came the faint sound of children's music. Adelene moved furtively along the tranquil street. Quiet voices flowed to her ears—chattering voices, evening laughter softly carried by the breeze. From somewhere among the clustered townhouses came the gentle clinking of silverware and wine glasses. Across the great Ceiling, stretching far above slept a grayish imitation of clouds as tranquil as the tombstones of the old church.

The girl walked on in the strange tranquility. A tiny Cleaner came wobbling out from somewhere among the buildings, inspecting the street here and there, the cold light from its diminutive eyes fixed on the ground before it. It hovered indifferently past her, fretfully buzzing and nattering to itself, and then it disappeared again, bumbling and sputtering among trash bins and discarded rubbish, as would a bee among flowers. It found a distorted soda can and went to examining it. The Cleaners were harmless little things.

I'm not safe here. Her heart hammered against her chest. An acute zapping sound tore through the silence and made her jump. *Don't scream, keep as quiet as possible. It's only a little noise.* A smoldered soda came clanking and tumbling towards her, and landed between her dirty shoes, sizzling and smoking. The Cleaner's silhouette floated out of the darkness again, snatched the can from between her legs, and vanished around the street corner.

Farther down, the tall houses turned along an irregular road. There passed the main boulevard, stretching past the southern outlet of Flemington, and reaching far into the Twenty-Eighth, to lose itself amid suburban paths. Down the other way, the boulevard stretched further still, up and beyond the northern outlet. There, it made its way among the wooded hills of the Thirtieth Division, shriveling slowly into rocky gravel. The mouth of transport channel bulged out from the boulevard, leading down below the sleeping streets into the Interdivision Metropolitan Complex. It was an endless network of subterranean lanes—passenger busses and private cars, TSA vessels and hybrid transportation droids—infinite lanes and platforms linked to ever town, every Division of the world; and yet isolated underground.

Adelene walked past the lonely shops and foggy windows, her pace quickening as darkness fell above the roofs. The glow of a streetlight mounted on a tall post at the entrance of the channel poured onto her visage. From beneath came the muffled sound of vehicles speeding along the lanes and the welcoming reverb of serene robotic voices over the amplifier. A man in a long black coat emerged from the hazy light below, moving hastily up the steps. His tall hat covered his eyes. He bumped into her as he passed under the lamppost, and mumbled something in the high collar of his coat. In an instant he was gone, taking the pattering of his hurried steps away with him.

It was cold. The girl tucked her hands into her shirt pockets.

"You should go home, you," a hoarse voice came from behind her. Adelene turned around. An aged woman stood next to her, bent laboriously on a wooden cane. Adelene had never seen an old woman before. Only the young and fit had been allowed to board the ship, to ensure that they would parent healthy children. It was imperative to minimize all threats to health and fertility across the three generations of habitants, the last of which would live to see the New World. Yet there were stories of old women who had passed as the guardians of young children and been granted the right to retire into the tranquil luxury of the *Inceptum Fidelis*. Perhaps this woman was one of them.

"Good evening, *domina*," Adelene said placidly, her breaths condensing into vapor in the cold night air.

"Hush! Hush." The arched old figure took two painful steps closer. Her florid fur coat was draped around her like a heavy mantle, shielding her from the lights, from time, from the youthful exuberance of the world. Under the shadow of a feathery hat, the small, wrinkled face, the pallid, pinched lips and crooked nose were pointed towards the girl. "Do you hear Them? Tell me, do you see Them?" A branch-like hand came to rest on Adelene's shoulder. "Old age has stolen precious senses from this wilting soul," the woman uttered, "Yet though I may not see or hear well, I can *feel* Them, yes. They're *everywhere!*" The woman raised her chin slightly as she spoke, and from beneath the large bonnet, dark and narrow eyes gleamed faintly in the light. Her words were slow, rhythmic, like the sway of long tree branches in the wind. Then, leaning closer to the girl's ears, a raucous whisper, words heaved from a breath of terror: "They're *looking* for someone."

"How do you mean, *domina?*" Adelene said, her voice agitated, her heart still pounding.

There was something of madness in the woman's ostentatious gesticulation, in the uncontrolled trembling of her hands, the rasping breaths and sunken voice. "Ah! Don't go down there," she hissed, looking down into the dimly lit station, "The night is agitated—something has *perturbed* Them. The Authorities have eyes in the back of their heads."

"Who are They looking for?" The girl's lips were dry with fear. *I need to get away from here.*

"They walk in *dozens* across the platform—I have seen Them," said the bent shadow, "Listen to me! You must not go down there—There has been some unlawful *infringement* somewhere in these parts. My old bones are quivering. You must be wary, dear child. Go home!" With these last words the dark cloak moved away slowly, grunting slightly after every conscientious step. Adelene followed the figure with her eyes and stood motionless. The girl felt her heart beat silently against her chest. It was *she* that They were after, and she was sure of it now. Somehow, They had all been informed.

The slow taping of the crooked cane echoed, echoed, and was gone.

Adelene's stomach ached with hunger. Hands tucked in her pockets, she too walked away from the light of the station's lamppost, and followed the boulevard towards the southern outlet. The Twenty-Sixth Division was four kilometers away. It was late, late in the night. The Ceiling had begun to split, noiselessly, slowly parting like immense shutters, and revealing the single great window that stretched from the East Wall to the West Wall, from the northern to the southern outlet…

It was a window opening onto Space itself—a crystalline surface behind which emerged the phantasmagoric multitude of lustrous stars scattered across the uncontainable universe. Below it the wallowing clouds hung like sleeping specters. Sometimes, if one paid no close attention to the exact distance between oneself and the clouds, to the way they came about, the way they moved below the Ceiling, to the reason why they rumbled when it rained, there was a certain sense of depth and form to them, and they looked very real indeed.

8 SYLVAN STRAYTOP

Sylvan Straytop kept a bee in a jar. It was a small, plumb bumblebee, with a missing leg. It had a furry smudge of orange on its back and a blur of white on its abdomen. Sylvan kept it on his desk, right below the window in his room. Its head was silky and black, save for a tuft of light brown hairs gathered between the large, beady eyes and twitching antennas.

It crawled funny, but that was because of the missing leg.

He never named it; he never felt the need to, because it didn't talk, and when he talked to it, it didn't listen. And he never mentioned it to anyone. Not like that was ever necessary either. Everyone knew Sylvan Straytop kept a bee in a jar.

9 SHADOWS

"Under the Lights, shadows never changed," the old man recounted. Your shadow would not stride behind you at morning nor rise to meet you at evening. You could sit beneath a tree for hours and hours, and the tree's shadow and all the shadows around you never stretched or shrunk, or moved very much at all. Time would feel as still as the shadows if you sat under a tree.

"Then when the Lights slowly faded, and the Ceiling quietly parted, and night settled onto the world, the shadows of the day disappeared, to reappear tranquil and untroubled the next morning. There was never much of anything under the shadows. Nothing really grew there. It was mostly dirt, and damp rocks with pill bugs under them. Most of the time They would grow artificial grass under the shadows so it wouldn't look too strange. It was called bogus grass, and it never yellowed. Not even in the winter.

"In our early school years, we played many games under the trees in the park. We would pick handfuls of grass from the field, and then handfuls of the artificial grass from the shadows, and we would make experiments on them. Sometimes we'd burn them, or place them in a bucket with muddy water and mash them into a strange purée, and other times we'd place snails on them and we'd watch the snails carefully as they munched on the bogus grass, expecting a peculiar change in their appearance or behavior. But none ever showed. Once, we even dared Joel to eat a clover growing in the shadow to see if it tasted different from normal clovers.

"*It tastes like lettuce*, he had said. *It tastes just like lettuce.* Otherwise you couldn't tell the difference.

"Giovanni wore his glasses everywhere he went because he was blind as a worm, so we would have him sit there and go through all the search results online. "Does it say anything?" we'd ask repetitively as he stared through the lenses at the blades of bogus grass. But the Internet didn't seem to notice any difference between normal grass and shadow grass.

"Then one summer Joel decided to feed his rabbit clovers just from under the trees. A week later the animal was so bony you could see its ribs under the brown fur. It didn't die, but it came close. There weren't any nutrients in the bogus grass. It only *looked* real. And it tasted like lettuce."

10 MYRNA

Heavy raindrops fell onto the Twenty Sixth division, whispering through the leaves of the trees and coating the damp grass with rainwater. They gleamed hazily under the gentle lights of the road. Adelene's footsteps made a light splashing sound against the wet pavement. In her head, the sound of the rain echoed, unceasing, forever repeating itself like the tick-tock of a timepiece. Her hair stuck to her face in thick strands, and water droplets slid down her reddened cheeks and dripped onto her coat. Her hands were buried in her pockets. She walked on, too tired to quicken her pace. Panicked by the old woman's words, she had decided to walk all the way home, but had not expected it to be so long. In the obscurity the houses seemed to blend with the landscape into one great cloud of night, and the air, stained with the droning sounds of the rain, carried an earthy smell.

All was silent. The night had not yet passed, and the small hamlet was asleep. Adelene crossed the path that led to the old grange by the field, and scurried along the quiet houses and gardens. Her socks felt wet inside her muddy shoes. The rain freckled the pond with tiny ripples, and the reeds along the bank rustled in a sudden gush of wind. She lived in a small house near the church. It had a wooden door with a brass doorknob and a small chime hanging above the welcome mat, and a narrow front yard with cherry trees that shaded the doorstep. The wall facing the terrace was made of high glass windows through which the Lights of day would illuminate the kitchen and living room. It was a white house with a pool. But all the houses were white. And they all had a pool.

The clouds rumbled above, blinding the stars as they loomed below the great window. The Ceiling had not yet begun to close out the stars. Adelene walked up the little path among the cherry trees. Panting, she wiped the water from her eyelashes and stood quietly behind the door. The edge of the slanted roof shielded her from the rain. At her approach, the lens of the eyehole shrunk with a low mechanical noise. In the corner below the roof, a small camera turned towards her and beeped softly, twice, three times.

"Myrna, its me," she whispered, looking up into the dark lens.

Footsteps sounded behind the door. Adelene stepped back. The low beeping came once more, and the wooden door opened, revealing Myrna's slender silhouette in the entryway. The lights of the living room turned on slowly.

The android stood with a hand against the open door, eyeing the girl with a cold glare. "Where were you, Miss Adelene?" she asked in a firm, placid tone.

"Please, Myrna, I'm exhausted. Let me in." Adelene said. It's something Sara had taught her. *If one of them asks you a question that you don't want to answer, give them a command, and they'll probably forget about it. At least for a while. That's how stupid they are.*

Myrna stepped aside without a word, watching the girl with the same coldness. Adelene walked silently into the relieving warmth of the room. She felt safe here. There was a welcoming smell of recently baked bread and carrot broth. It was always carrot broth.

"Where are your contacts, Miss Adelene?"

"I lost them." The girl stepped out of her dirty shoes. A Cleaner scurried out from behind the kitchen counter and crankily wobbled up to her. The tiny automaton greeted her with a withdrawn nod of the head, and then ran off across the room carrying the mud-stained shoes.

"You know how unsafe that is," Myrna said, "How did you lose them?"

"Myrna, I'm sorry, I—They were bothering me. My eyes were itchy, so I took them out," she lied, "I don't remember where I left them. You can get me new ones tomorrow." She took a seat at the counter, her eyes avoiding Myrna's. "Is Mom home yet?" she asked, to break the silence that had followed.

"No," Myrna answered. The reflection of the ceiling lights moved smoothly up her mechanical arm as she handed the girl a glass of water.

Adelene gulped down the water thirstily but did not ask for a plate of carrot broth. It was far past dinnertime, and Myrna would never allow it. Adelene had never really liked Myrna. Sometimes she wished things could be as they were before, when her father was still with them. Outside, the rain whispered in the trees.

Myrna walked across the room and along the glass wall speckled in raindrops, then into the small room behind the dining table. Adelene watched the lean figure disappear into the shadows.

Adelene yawned, passed a hand through her wet hair and stepped off the stool. She left the kitchen and walked lazily up the stairs. Slowly, the scents of the kitchen faded away. She wondered if Lành was asleep yet. Usually he had trouble going to bed when their mother was away. This time, as Adelene had been told, she had gone to Filmur, the

Sixth Division for a few days. Some habitants had been complaining about the new Curriculum at the Secondary School. She was an Aide for the Judicial Authorities, but such a job did not bring many benefits to the family, let alone make them Privileged. Fine restaurants and the best theaters remained almost inaccessible, especially on holidays, and so were the best neighborhoods, homes and private vehicles. Her children still had to give up their seats on the train or bus when a Privileged family stepped in. Yet perhaps one day His Excellency the Onweald would grant her Recognition. Their mother was by nature a conscientious and hard-working woman who could not spend her days sitting in a chair knitting or writing. She needed a professional lifestyle, a gratifying feeling to accompany her on a daily basis, and ambition to lead her on.

She had been gone for five days now, and Lành cried himself to sleep every night. Only once had his mother managed to lull him to sleep through the hologram. Every night he would watch her silhouette materialize from the light beams projected from the communication system, and she would sit next to him on his little bed and tell him that she'd be home soon. Then she'd say goodnight and blow him a kiss, and disappear again. He was worried about losing her. He was scared that she'd leave him like their father had.

Adelene opened the door to Lành's room, just enough for the light to seep onto the boy's face.

"Adelene?" she heard him say. Lành could see her silhouette in the doorway. Between the gritty darkness of the bedroom and the light of the hallway, she seemed a shadow without a source. She walked into the room and came to sit on the edge of her brother's bed.

"Lành, you should be sleeping. It's really late," she said. Her clothes were still wet from the rain, and, noticing this, she stood back up from the bed and instead pulled a small chair from under her brother's desk, brought it to the edge of the bed and sat on it."

"Where were you? Where's Olio?" the little voice asked, "I don't like it when I'm alone with Myrna." "I know, I know. Sorry," Adelene said.

He stirred under the covers. "I didn't get to say goodnight to Mommy."

"Why not?"

"Myrna didn't let me turn the hologram on. She says I'm an irresponsible child. I should learn to have more respect for what the Authorities say."

"Why? What did you do?"

Lành lowered his voice down to a cautious whisper. "She told me to go to bed, and I started pouting about it. So now she won't let me talk to Mommy. She says I'm punished."

Adelene sighed. "It's O.K," she said, "I'm here now. And Mommy will be back soon." She looked around the room, almost expecting to find Myrna watching them. "She's right, you know," she continued, "We owe Them a lot of respect. Look at how well Myrna looks after us both. The Authorities are the Onweald's agents, here to protect us all, to make sure every single one of us has the comfort needed to live a happy life. On Earth, there are thieves, poor people and wars. People disobey their governments. People die every day of sickness. We have to be thankful that we don't have any of this here. His Excellency The Onweald makes sure of that. We are all blessed."

Lành nodded halfheartedly. He had heard this said so many times.

"Go to sleep, Lành," Adelene added, "I'll see you in the morning." She kissed him on the cheek and rose.

Lành said nothing. Eyes half-closed, he watched his sister tiptoe out of the room. Before closing the door behind her, she turned around and said, "Remember what I told you. Be thankful for all you have," and she smiled.

It was silent inside the house now. The Cleaners had long since finished their daily cleanups in the kitchen and bathrooms, and Myrna had probably deactivated herself for the night, motion sensor and sound recorder left on, as it was every night. The rain had ceased as well. As Adelene stepped into her room, her eyes wondered out the window and were met with the cloudy remnant of a rainy sky. No, it wasn't the sky, of course, but how it looked like it! The stars, the clouds, the night. If one doesn't call this the sky than what does one call it? It was just that. And yet it wasn't. Not at all. There were no more than seventy-eight meters separating the houses of every division from the upper limit. At night it was a window that watched the stars, and in the daytime it was a ceiling that locked them out.

She flopped down on her bed, her body sore from the weight of the day's events. The sheets felt soothing against her skin. Her mind was blank from drowsiness, and she could not think, not even about Olio. Without her contact lenses she had no idea of the time, but it felt good not to have them on. Once Adelene was online, Myrna could tell exactly where she was at every second of the day. Whatever she looked up through her lenses, Myrna kept a record of. Sometimes, the contact lenses would give her information on the most random things—a tree, an insect, a vehicle on the road—without her asking. The elaborate description would appear in front of her and then disappear once the object of focus left her field of vision. There were other times when she would be lost in thought, and her contacts would immediately display in front of her eyes an array of definitions related to her thoughts. Sometimes it came in handy, but most of the time it bothered her.

An owl hooted somewhere in the dark. Then suddenly

there came a sound from behind the window, and Adelene gasped. She sat up abruptly. To her relief, the figure in the window was not that of an android. In the darkness, the face was hazy and indistinguishable, but someone—a person—was crouched behind the window, motioning her to open it. Adelene stepped out of the bed and walked cautiously up to the windowsill. She commanded the lights to turn on, but without her contacts she could not send a Thought Signal, and the darkness stayed.

"Sara?" she whispered. She opened the window hastily. "Sara, what are you doing here?"

"Mind if I come in?" the figure said. Her face was clearer now. She was standing on the roof that jutted from the side of the house, above the dining room. She squeezed her way through the open window before Adelene could give an answer. Once inside she wiped the humidity off her forehead and looked for a place to sit. The rain had curled and darkened her long brown hair. "I gotta talk to you," she said, "Is your babbler awake?"

"I don't think so."

Sara called Them babblers. *Because that's what they do all day*, she would explain, *they babble on about what we should and should not do, should and should not say. Talkative little idiots.* Sara's lips were red from the cold and her face pale, but she was pretty like that. Adelene always found Sara prettier than her. Sara was an orphan, raised in the Sanctuary since she was three years old. For all those years she had felt like a wild bird cooped up in a cage, and since she was thirteen had avoided the place as much as possible, going back only to eat and sleep. Soon enough the Nurses had given up going after her.

"Can you turn the light on for a minute?" Sara asked.

When she saw Adelene walk up to the switch on the wall Sara gave her a puzzled look. "What are you doing? What happened to your contacts?"

"Lost 'em."

Sara chuckled. "Yeah, right. That might work when you're talking to the android, but not to me. Come on, what did you do."

"We can't talk here, Sara."

Sara ignored her. "I told you those things were annoying, the contacts and glasses. They want us to wear them all the time, but honestly I don't see the point. I bet they just enjoy *stalking* us." Saying this she raised both hands in front of her, making clawing motions at the air, the way the Big Bad Wolf from children's stories did.

"Sara, be quiet! Myrna could hear you."

"Oh, I'm scared!"

"It's not funny."

"You're right. It's *not*," Sara acquiesced in a sarcastic tone, "It's just that they like keeping an eye on their precious little pets, *don't* they? Need to make sure the humans don't do anything *silly*, because—What if one of us gets *hurt*? Oh *no*! How could their little emotionless faces survive the *shock*?" And she laughed.

Adelene looked at her coldly. "Sara, if you get arrested, don't drag me along with you. Please."

"What!" Sara said with exaggerated incredulity, "You mean for sedition? I'm not seditious; I'm just a bit more talkative than most people. Besides, I can't get arrested. I'm too quick for them. They'll get tired of chasing me." She sniggered. "So, how was Flemington? Lily saw you there with that robot you stole."

"I didn't steal anything!"

"Then who's the little golem I saw following you around the other day? Don't tell me the thing is yours."

"Yes he is! His name's Olio. That's what Lành named him." Her voice was so low she wasn't sure Sara could hear her anymore. "We've had him for years, but now that my father's gone, I'm not even sure we're supposed to keep him. But we really love him, especially Lành."

"But if he's government property, of course the Authorities want him back! Does Myrna know?"

"He avoids her as best he can, but she doesn't pay attention to him. Usually he stays upstairs with me or Làhn."

"But Myrna's your Familiar! You mean to say she just *ignores* him?"

"No, you don't understand. Olio's been in the family since I was born. My father worked in the Laboratories but he worked from home a lot, bringing the robots in and working on them on dining room table. Olio was one of his long-term projects and we got used to having him around the house. Then when our father passed away, Olio made me swear I wouldn't take him back to the Laboratories. It was against the Law, but as long as we kept him hidden from the Police no one would know."

"That thing is from Laboratories?" Sara whispered incredulously. "Seriously? Adelene, I can't believe you never told me about this! Where is he now?"

"We separated a few hours ago and I have no idea where he is. I just hope he didn't get caught..."

"What the hell were you doing in Flemington?"

"I said I can't talk about it here, Sara."

"Oh, come on! She can't hear you!"

"What if she can?"

"She's deactivated."

"Yeah, but she keeps her recorder on at night."

"You're no fun, Addie," Sara continued jokingly. There came a small noise from downstairs and both of them kept quiet for a long while, until it was certain that the house was silent again. "Well, you're right, I better go now, before your babbler decides to shoot me." She climbed back through the window soundlessly.

"Wait! Hold on! What did you want to tell me?" asked

Adelene.

Sara turned around and stuck her face partially through the open window. "Right. Don't tell anyone this obviously, but Hacker found this place in the Twenty-First," she whispered, "It's some sort of old barn they don't use anymore. Once or twice a week you get a few picnickers who pass through but they usually stay on the paths. And its completely Microbot-free. Literally."

"How do you know?"

"Hacker."

"How does *he* know?"

"Adelene, you know the kid, he's a genius. He just *knows*. Meet me at the school around ten o'clock Sunday morning. We'll get to talk more about your little excursion to Flemington." She grinned slightly, her pupils large and black under the lightless sky. The girl moved stealthily to the far end of the roof and jumped to the ground without a sound. And then her shadow, formed by the scattered glow of the lone streetlight that reached above the trees, mingled with those of the bushes and undergrowth that lined the road.

11 GLASS WALLS

The bee had everything it wanted in the jar. Sylvan gave it honey and chunks of sugar, and fresh flowers, and water in an upturned bottle cap. There were holes in the silver cap, small holes to let the air in. One day he left the jar open and the bee flew out the window and it disappeared across the lake, and away into the pasture beyond, and it never came back.

The light of day reflected off the glass walls of the empty jar and Sylvan sat in a small wooden chair and looked into it. He saw his face reflected too, silently stretched inside the glass like a long shadow. The bee was happy in the jar. Why would it escape and never come back?

The next day he had a new one, and he made himself believe it was the old one, and that it had come back after all.

12 GONE

Adelene's mother had a quiet disposition. She was extremely reserved and rather shy. She was a loving mother, kind, affectionate and caring. Her name was Jade. Ace had loved her more than the world, and it was with her that he had left Earth. She loved him too, with all her heart, because he had an exceptional heart. He was a resilient young man with a strong will and force of character that rose above all else. He had left for the sake of their love, because it was something that he would never abandon. On the *Inceptum Fidelis*, there was no one to tell them what to do, and they felt safe. They were given a Familiar and a beautiful home. When Adelene was born, two years into the voyage, they felt suddenly grounded to the ship by the force of family. The ship was their home—their new world—forever. This had been true ever since the departure of the transportation aircrafts that took them from Earth to M.A.R.S. Orbital Protectorate 002, where the ship had been constructed, on February 14, 2109— *"Are you afraid?* Ace had asked Jade on the day of the Great Departure. And when she had not answered he had said, *"Hold my hand, Jade. We can't go back now. This is it."*—Yet it was only two years into the voyage that the truth unreservedly took hold of them. They would live among the stars, everywhere and yet nowhere at all, floating forever through the immensity of the universe.

Lành was four years old when Ace was taken from their lives. Adelene had just turned twelve. It was in the summer. She remembered that day as clearly as she would a haunting nightmare. It was lodged deep in her mind, and sometimes it did come back to her in her sleep, harsh waves of unburied thoughts flowing into her mind on agitated nights.

"I have something to show you, Adelene," her father said to her, taking her by the hand and helping her up the latter into the attic. Before going up the latter, his eyes darted warily about the house, as if he did not want to be seen. Adelene was scared of the attic, because it was very dark and gloomy, and full of spider webs. It reminded her of Myrna's closet, behind the dinning room. It wasn't as scary when her father was there with her. She watched him fumble around in the darkness under the low roof and pull out a brown cardboard box. He heaved it out of a pile of other old things—a computer, a pile of worn-down toys, broken Cleaners and deactivated dust-droids—and placed it in front of Adelene.

"What is it?" she asked, sitting down on the floor in front of the box and placing her hand on it to feel its rough texture.

"It's a really special box that I brought here from Earth."

"What's in it?" Adelene smiled with enthusiasm, tugging at the rough flaps fastened down with tape.

Ace looked down at the opening in the floor through which they had come. The light reflected in his pensive eyes. "Memories," he said. And with a melancholy smile he added, "They're for you. And when Lành is old enough, you will pass them on to him." He took out a small cutting tool and passed the blade across the wrapping tape and let Adelene open the box.

Inside was a thin white screen, wrapped in a bundle of woven fabric. Adelene gently slipped her hand into the box and picked it up. How light it was! She passed her fingers across the smooth surface. "How does it work?" she asked.

"Put on your glasses and command it to turn on."

"Do I *have* to put my glasses on for this?" At the time, she didn't like wearing her glasses, because she didn't like seeing the world in words. She didn't like the definitions that always appeared in front of her eyes whenever she looked at an object, as if there was only one way to define a rock, one way to define a person, one way to define the stars.

Her father smiled. "Only to send the thought signal," he said, "This is a special object. It's a secret object. What you will see, your eyes and your mind are free to interpret as they wish."

Adelene was somewhat puzzled, but curiosity made her lips curve into an eager smile, and she fit the glasses over her nose.

Turn on, she thought. An array of light flickered from the device and after quivering and sputtering for some time a three-dimensional image formed, projected between the screen and the lenses of her glasses. It was an image of a vast body of water that seemed to never end. The image moved. Adelene could see the waves glistening and thrashing about, and she could hear them, too. The soft sounds of the deep blue water in the image from the screen captivated her. Suddenly, from the water leaped a gigantic creature, tearing through the air with unrepressed beauty. Behind it was the Sky, defined against the brilliant blue of the water as if the image was split in two. There was the water, and there was the Sky, and both were everlasting. As enchantingly as it had jumped out, the great whale plunged back into the water with a splash of such force that the waves shot up into foam and fell back in translucent drops of water.

"It's beautiful, Daddy," Adelene mumbled, in awe, "It's so beautiful."

"It is a film about the ocean. I told you about the ocean."

Adelene smiled. "It's the most beautiful thing I have ever seen!"

"It is magical."

"Is it really true?"

Ace had feared that question. "Is what true, honey?"

"Is it true that there is a place like this on Earth?"

Her father seemed hesitant to answer. It was dark in the attic, but Adelene could see tears glistening in his eyes, in the light of the opening, where the latter was. Then finally he said, "Yes. Yes it is." He stroked her hair. "And I want you to have the memories too. I want you to know the world you are from."

Adelene looked up at him. "Are there more films?"

"Yes, there are many more. Some of them are stories, too. They are all in here. This is something I treasure a lot. Now it is yours to keep because you are very grown up now."

"Daddy, why did you leave Earth?"

For a moment he was silent, and then he smiled and kissed her on the cheek. "Adelene," he said with a soft yet serious voice. Adelene liked the serious voice, because it made her feel like she was treated like an adult. "This journey that you and I are part of, and to which all of us now have an obligation, is one of the greatest and most selfless steps—if not *the* greatest—in the history of humanity. We are heading towards this New World to colonize its land, and to harness a source of clean and powerful energy that, when shipped back to Earth, would help billions of people. It is an honorable thing, what we have chosen to do, for the sake of humanity."

But I didn't chose, Daddy, Adelene wanted to say, *I didn't chose to live my whole life on the ship.* But she only nodded, and smiled lovingly. He kissed her on the cheek.

"And most importantly," her father added, *"you* are my treasure now. You, Lành and your mother are far more important to me than the world would ever be."

She knew what he meant. Had her parents not left Earth, they would have been torn from one another, forcefully, cruelly, forever. And Adelene and Lành would never have been born.

That night, when everyone was asleep and the house was silent, Adelene put on her glasses and sat up under her covers, and then she slipped the little screen between her crossed legs and told it to turned on and play a movie for her. This time, it was not the image of the ocean, and the great blue whale, and the cloudless sky. But, just as vast and continuous as that ocean and that sky had been, so were the sand dunes that stretched out of the screen and plunged into her sight. The wind blew onto the crests and washed the sand into the thin desert air. And then the image changed and she was moving among a crowd of men and large beige and brown animals with drooping snouts and long necks. The animals had a large bump on their backs and strange-looking feet. The men and the women wore long robes and cloths wrapped around their heads to protect them from the heat of the sun that stabbed the earth from somewhere up above. On the backs of the animals were loads of goods that had been hauled and fastened there, rolled-up carpets and blankets, and long sticks of wood for building tents. Some of the animals and men were sitting down, and far, far in the vast landscape there were shrubs and palm trees growing in the sand. There was a little naked boy in the image, and his skin was very dark and there was sand in his hair and on his feet, and he was running between the legs of the animals, and he was playing with a stick. She could hear the voices speaking in a strange language, and the low-pitched groans and bellows of the beige-brown animals, and the soft howl of the wind in the dunes. Then, involuntarily, Adelene began to close her eyes, and the sounds of the encampment in the desert lulled her to sleep.

Every night, Adelene watched watch the moving pictures of the Earth. Over and over again. They were all beautiful. There were stories about love, bravery, and about happiness. There were stories about war and poverty, and of people who found happiness no matter where they found themselves. Sometimes, she closed her eyes because the images were scary. Other times, she had trouble closing her eyes, or even blinking, for fear of missing a single detail. She was mesmerized, fascinated, and stupefied by the magic of it all. One night, the story was set far north, where there is always snow, and she was flying over the tips of countless snow-covered mountains, in a landscape of clouds. They were real clouds—not like the clouds above her own home—real clouds that formed as high up as the tips of the mountains and washed over her in the three-dimensional film. The air was so clear that the cliffs and the snow looked as though they had sliced the sky into rugged mountains, and the cold sun made the snow glisten on their icy faces.

I'm flying! Adelene smiled, her eyes gleaming with pleasure, *I'm flying in the Sky!* She took a deep breath. She could almost smell the freshness of the snow and feel the coldness of the air. She wanted to stretch her arms out and plunge down among the mountains. She wanted to caress the world with her own hands, free as the rays of the sun.

That night, Myrna was standing in the doorway. She stood watching, her tall slender figure dark against the light of the hallway behind her. She walked silently towards Adelne's bed, a small syringe in her hand. Her blue eyes gleamed like lasers in the sleeping darkness.

"Adelene," the android said, with calm firmness. The girl gasped under the covers and the music from the film ceased. Mryna reached her hand out and pulled back the covers, revealing the small white screen in Adelene's hands. "What is this, dear girl?"

Adelene did not answer.

"Give it to me, Adelene," Myrna ordered.

Adelene's heart was pounding with anxiety. "No, Myrna. It's mine." She hugged the screen against her chest and did not look up.

Myrna was silent for some time, and then she moved closer, widened her eyes and passed her laser scanner across the screen.

"No!" Adelene whimpered, "Leave me alone!"

Myrna looked at her coldly. "Who gave this to you, Adelene?" she asked. When the girl refused to respond, she added, "You are being very disobedient. I am sure your mother would be very disappointed if I told her how disrespectful you were to your House Domestic."

"Oh, please, Myrna! Don't tell my parents I watch the films at night!" Adelene begged, finally looking up at Myrna.

"Well, then, do as I ask. Answer me. Who gave you this visual transmitter?"

"Daddy gave it to me," Adelene mumbled.

"Your father?"

"Yes," she said, tightening her grip around the smooth edges of the screen, "It's mine now."

"Hand it over to me now, honey," Myrna's voice echoed.

Adelene hesitated. "Promise you will give it back to me?"

"Of course I will. But I do not want you to sleep with it." She held out her hand.

Reluctantly, Adelene handed her the screen. "Promise?"

"I promise." Myrna came to sit at the edge of the bed. "Now, lie down and hold out your arm like this."

Adelene obeyed quietly. She held out her arm along the soft bedcover, palm facing up. Myrna held the arm with one hand and placed a cold finger onto the large vein in at the start of the girl's forearm, below the elbow. In the other hand she held the tiny syringe. In the darkness of the room, Adelene couldn't see the needle at the end.

"What are you doing?" she asked with a tired voice.

"This will help you sleep," Myrna answered with a soft voice as she carefully stuck the needle under the skin in Adelene's forearm. "It shoos out all the bad thoughts in your mind and replaces them with good thoughts."

The girl withdrew slightly from the pain, but it went away as quickly as it had come. "That hurts a little."

Myrna pressed onto the end of the syringe to let the liquid inside flow out slowly. "There we go," she said, taking the needle out and pressing her finger on the tiny wound. "That wasn't too bad, was it?"

Adelene shook her head.

"Good. Now go to sleep, my dear. I will see you in the morning." Myrna said, walking gracefully back to the door. "Goodnight."

Adelene slipped her arm back under the covers and turned to her side. "Goodnight," she rejoined.

The next morning, she found her mother sitting at the kitchen counter with her face in her hands. When she raised her head, her cheeks were stained with tears and her eyes were wide and full of fear.

"What's wrong, Mom?" Adelene asked. The strange fear in her mother's eyes flowed into hers. "Where is Dad?"

"Daddy won't be here with us anymore for a while,

honey," Jade said with a quavering voice. Her hands were trembling.

"I don't understand," Adelene said in a frail tone. "Why won't he be living with us anymore?"

Her mother hid her face with her hand again and started blankly out the glass wall of the living room. "It would be too difficult for you to understand, Adelene. You're not old enough. When you get older, you will understand."

Adelene's voice quivered. Tears rose to her eyes and blurred her vision. "Is Daddy gone forever, Mommy?"

Jade looked up at her. Her eyes, reddened with tears, held in them a deep and tormenting sadness. Her lips moved slightly, but no sound came, as if the sorrow chocked her words. She seemed unsure what to say. And finally with a frail hand she took her daughter's small hand in hers. "Yes, sweetheart," she said with a torn voice, "Daddy's gone."

The words tore through Adelene's heart like knives. She never forgot those words.

The screen with the films was gone too, but Adelene never noticed. The night before, the screen and the images had slowly fallen from her mind. Perhaps the images hadn't fallen, and had instead been pushed out by force, but whatever had happened did not matter, because she did not remember.

Sometimes, on agitated nights, the memory of that morning comes back to her in her sleep like a nightmare, but the screen with the moving images had left her memory the way some dreams are forgotten and never remembered. That day, from the corner of the living room wall, where the first floor hallway started, Myrna watched the mother and the daughter, and she was silent. She held the empty syringe in her hand.

13 NIGHTMARE

Sometimes, at night, when Pam is lying in her bed and the house is quiet, and not even the night birds sing in the shadows, the memories come back. Sounds echo in the little girl's ears. She hears the silent cries of her mother mingled with the incessant blaring of the sirens, the frightened voices calling her name, falling upon her as the darkness falls, lingering in her mind like fog over the hushed waters of a lake. The memories hurt—they sting—the way pavement scorched by the midday sun used to sting under her bare feet. She remembers the policemen, forcing her father's hands behind his back, pulling her mother away from her, grabbing Pam's own skinny arm with strong fingers and carrying her, like a burden, in their forceful arms. It was dark. So dark. And the lights from the sirens on the police cars enveloped the night in trenchant flashes of red and blue.

"Mommy!" She hears herself cry, deep in her mind, "Mommy! Daddy!"

How old was she that day, so long ago, when the men took them away? Was it past her birthday? How long had it been since she had last eaten a full meal? For many weeks, before, her life had been the road. Everyday her family would walk, on an on in the wilderness, along the arid roads and deserted villages, hiding at night, hiding in the forests, the abandoned shacks—always hiding—and always walking.

"Where do we walk to now, Daddy?" Faintly, the quiet words whispered to her father—the echoes of her own little voice—wash over her, a doleful melody rustling like the wind in the leaves.

"We are walking West," the father would answer, "As far West as possible. Where you will be safe, you and your brother. All of us."

"Will we have a house where we are going?" her brother asked her once. She still remembers the trust with which the little boy held her hand as they walked, holding on as if she were all the strength in the world, all the comfort he could ever find, combined in one little girl with bare feet.

"Of course we will," she would pant, squeezing his tiny hand, "Mommy told me we'll find someone to help us hide, so that the men in the uniforms don't catch us. If they catch us, they'll bring us back. And Mommy says we *can't* go back home. We *can't*, you know. It's too dangerous there now."

And then she shuts her eyes and presses her hands against her ears, and the memories go away. They come to rest on the windowsill, quiet, distant, watching her as she falls asleep. The owl yawns under the fainted Lights. In the room across the hall, the little boy sleeps soundly, a velvety teddy bear in his arms. Slowly, the tranquility of the night comes back.

The policemen didn't send her back. They didn't send any of them back. They interrogated them, they watched the father beg and the mother cry, they presented them with the options, they gave them a choice. It was either deportation, or joining the 300,000 others boarding the

Inceptum Fidelis, the great spaceship bound for a Faraway World, scheduled to depart on the twentieth day of the second month of the year 2109. Their children would live a tranquil life without sickness, without poverty or war. They would live in luxury, and there was nothing to give up, other than the world they knew. They would never see the Earth again. None of them ever would. They gave up the world for their children, because there was nothing else left to give up.

14 MIDDLETON SCHOOL

The School of Middleton was only a quarter of an hour away from Adélene's house by foot. She always walked to school. It was a quiet Sunday afternoon, but she found it much safer for her to travel above ground, by foot, rather than in a vehicle of any sort driven by one of Them. The Authorities had probably looked for her all night in the Twenty-Ninth Division, and who knew whether They had given up yet? She walked down the road with her hands in her pockets and her eyes cast down at the ground. A Gardener carrying large flower bouquets in its arms crossed her path and almost bumped into her.

"Sorry," she mumbled halfheartedly, barely looking up.

The Cleaners, Gardeners and Merchants were all somewhat inoffensive, held a rather pathetic place in Society and were rather small-minded, but still procured some level of respect from humans. There was no insulting a Gardener nor kicking a Cleaner into a gully, although doing so had no particular consequence other than perhaps losing the favor of a neighbor who had witnessed the ungrateful act. Oftentimes it was advised not to mess with such Service Robots simply because it was in one's best interest not to upset a Service Robot. Nobody really knew why. It was part of the Law and no one questioned the Law. Daring habitants would sometimes whisper, in the deceivingly safe ambience of their own homes, that Service Robots were part of "the thousand eyes of the Centrum Solis," secretly on the lookout for suspicious meetings or signs of subversion or thievery, which were all Central crimes. But it did not matter very long, what those habitants said, because soon such persons went missing and no one ever ask nor even wondered where they were, because things seemed better that way. Things were better when no one questioned or disturbed.

Adelene stared down at her feet and hummed a tune under her breath. On such Sundays in springtime, the streets of the village were full of small children playing and giggling on the roads, along the paths and in the parks. There were always two or three Nurses holding the hands of the younger ones, watching out for bikers or horses. All the young children had glasses or contact lenses, because when school was closed, they continued to learn and grow on their own, and needed to see the world in the good way of Society, with all the information they needed laid flat in front of their eyes. Adelene crossed the village square and walked down the path between flowering trees that led to the school building. There were shutters on the many long, arched windows of the lavish two-story edifice, opening onto the gardens.

"There you are!" Sara exclaimed as Adelene reached the end of the path. Sara was leaning against one of the large, neatly arranged trees that grew at the edge of the well-kept aggregate of small white stones that formed the path. "Thought you had given up on me. Thought you were going to let me rot here in this dreadful place all by myself."

"Sorry," Adelene said, panting. "I decided to walk here,

and it took me a while, I know."

"Mm-hm," she acquiesced, and nudged herself off the tree with her elbow. She walked towards Adelene nonchalantly. "So, where's you're clanky fellow?"

Adelene looked over her shoulder, her eyes scrutinizing the surroundings. Nothing moved, and there was nothing to hear, save the chirping of birds high up in the trees, and the gentle falling of a fountain into its stone basin somewhere in the periphery of the school. They were alone. "He hasn't come back," Adelene answered finally, "It's been two days now. Do you think he could've gotten caught?"

"I don't know," Sara said, her voice more serious than before. *Probably*, her eyes said.

"What should we do?"

"Well, for now, let's just hope he *didn't* get caught. Come with me." She took her by the hand and stole around the silent walls and along the rows of trimmed shrubs and bushes to the back of the building. There was a low wooden door in the wall, buried under a mass of overgrown vines and leafy plants. It was difficult to push open, but the Teachers never locked it. It was of no particular use. It was simply another way to the basement where the Primary School's art rooms were. On weekdays, there were no more than three or four Teachers there, waiting for their scheduled classes. And on weekends there were never more than one or two, simply there for surveillance.

The two girls tiptoed down the empty hallway without a sound. Faint rays of daylight seeped through the windows in the classrooms, but the place was dark and rather dusty.

"This way," Sara said, leading Adelene to one of the doors.

"Don't just barge into a random classroom, Sara!" Adelene whispered apprehensively, holding her friend back.

"I'm just checking to see if it's open. Don't worry, there's no one down here. I know it sounds strange, but I came with Hacker yesterday and we expected to see one or two babblers somewhere around, keeping watch, but there was absolutely no one."

"How's that even possible?"

"I don't know."

Suddenly, the low door through which they had come in opened violently and a bright string of light poured into the hallway. Then it was dark again. The two girls squeezed together in the corner between the classroom door and the wall and stood motionless against it, holding their breaths. Sara placed her hand on Adelene's mouth to keep her quiet, and they waited. Footsteps, heavy and inhuman, resounded through the school basement and seemed to come closer and closer. *It's just a Teacher*, Adelene thought to herself, *It's just a Teacher*. The Teacher passed by, but the blue lights of its eyes did not fall onto them. It was mumbling to itself fretfully as it passed, its back bent slightly forward and its hands clasped together behind it.

"*Find 3254Z9X0...Escaped...Not Found...Find it; seek, look, find, take back,*" it murmured, "*Find 3254Z9X0. Attention. Attention. His Excellency. Operation Z9X0 87327. Find. Capture. 87327.*"

The android turned to face one of the classroom doors, entered the password in the laser number orb that floated above the doorknob and barged into the room. Inside, the strange murmurings continued. "*g-negative... 87327 g-negative... Report security breach... section 911482... Attention.*" The strange speech seemed to come from some sort of radio transmitter, hostile and mechanical, and yet it was the android itself that mouthed the words. Adelene had never heard a Teacher speak this way. It was eerie, almost frightening. All of the mimicry of human behavior that was usually present in the Teachers' comportment was utterly gone and the android did not walk like a human or comport itself like one. It was a grotesque humanoid lacking grace and posture, mind and reason. The two girls remained immobile in the shadows, Sara squeezing Adelene's hand. For the first time, the robotic nature of the Authorities stared them in the face, naked and disclosed, and Adelene felt a whirr of fear in her heart.

There was a series of noises inside the open classroom. A desk was moved around, a pencil fell to the ground and then the slender metallic figure stormed out of the room, and hurried back down the hallway. The sound of its steps fell, and fell, and was heard no more. There was another flash of daylight, again the sound of the small door screeching as it closed, and then darkness. And then silence.

Sara slowly let go of Adelene's hand.

"Is she gone?" Adelene whispered.

"I think so," came the quiet answer, "She left the door open. Let's go."

"You want to go in there?"

"Where else do you want to go? Back out *there*? I say we're stuck here for another hour or so. Who knows how many more of Them are crawling around the place." Sara walked cautiously to the other side of the hallway, pulling Adelene along. They passed through the doorway and into the small classroom, and Sara closed the door behind them. It was warmer in the room. There was an android standing immobile in the back.

Adelene gasped, but Sara reassured her. "That one's deactivated," Sara said calmly. When Adelene did not respond, she walked up to the inert figure, gave it a strong push and watched it stumble stupidly to the ground. "See? Turned off. Dead as a doornail."

There were children's drawings on the walls, displayed creatively between the long arched windows that illuminated the room. Sara walked casually up to one of the drawings. "Look at what this kid drew," she said, laughing a little. It was a clumsy circle painted green and blue, with a large yellow orb drawn next to it. The yellow orb had long, irregular lines coming out of it in all directions. "It's the Earth, and I guess that's the Sun. Cute, isn't it?"

"How long do you think we have before the Teacher comes back?" Adelene asked, her voice still uneasy.

"I doubt she'll come back at all. She seemed in a hurry. It was weird, what she was saying. Did you hear any of it?"

"Yes. Well, no. I didn't really get what that was about. I had never heard one of Them talk like that before."

"She was under some sort of orders, that's for sure. *Security breach*, she said. I wonder what that's about." Sara walked to the Teacher's desk and sat in the chair insouciantly.

"Sara, I have to tell you something."

Sara looked up as if she were about to receive the first interesting piece of information of the day. "What?"

"It's about the other day."

"Right, tell me about it." Sara leaned forward, her chin in her palms and her elbows on the desk.

"With Olio."

"Uh-huh."

"In Flemington."

"Yeah. I know. Come on, get on with it, Addie." She took out a piece of chewing-gum from a pack in her pocket and popped it in her mouth. "This is way too suspenseful for me."

"Yeah but this is important! I think those orders had to do with me."

"What? No," Sara laughed, "I know that whole thing with the robot on the lose got you super anxious and everything, but you gotta remember that you're not actually *implicated*. They can't think your father's been helping him hide, because he's dead. And they surely wouldn't think the android *itself* begged anyone to keep it safe, because all robots are programmed to Obey. If worse comes to worst, you could easily convince them it ran away on its own—short-circuited or something—and you're just an innocent little human girl who happened to find him and decided to keep him as a pet. Was that a good idea? No. Actually, it was an incredibly *stupid* idea. But just the fact that they're looking for him is reassuring. It means he hasn't been caught yet and is probably hiding somewhere. And as long as They don't know for sure that someone's been helping him hide, there's nothing to worry about."

"But They *do* know!" Adelene blurted out.

"What?"

"They know someone's been hiding him! They probably think I have him right now!"

"How the hell did They find out?"

Adelene told her about the restricted areas behind the Universal Library, the vaulted passageways past the Walls of Flemington, the gigantic, cold room full of emergency escape vessels. She explained how Olio had modified one of them for her, and how he had presented it as a surprise, without realizing what he was getting her into. She explained how they had escaped when suddenly the alarm had rung—how she had convinced Olio to break through the door—and how they ended up separating in the maze of dark corridors. She described how abnormally silent the streets of Flemington were once she stumbled back out, and she told her about old woman who advised her not to go down into the Metropolitan Complex that night. It was better to stay out of the way of the Authorities, the woman had said, because there had been an 'infringement' somewhere around, and anyone could become suspect. She told her how she finally managed to get home safely, by foot, in the rain. It was after all of this that Sara had appeared at the window to talk to her, and that she had unfortunately left after a shorter conversation than she had expected.

Sara did not interrupt her once. She listened on, wide-eyed and mouth partly open in disbelief. When Adelene finally fell silent, there was a long pause. Sara turned her chewing-gum around in her mouth with her tongue and stared pensively out in front of her, as if her eyes had been frozen in that position. She seemed to watch her own thoughts pass by. Then she blinked and looked at Adelene. "Holy shit, Adelene," she said calmly, "Holy *shit*."

15 WANTED

"So now the Police is after you," Sara said, "That's nice." Sara leaned back in her chair and flicked an ant off her shoulder. "I thought you were in enough trouble stealing robots."

"I didn't *steal* Olio!" Adelene retorted, "Stop putting it that way."

"Oh, I'm sorry, Addie. How should I put it? 'My friend here keeps an Independently-Monitored Laboratory Automaton—official and permanent property of the Governmental Authorities—in her attic, with many other kooky toys of the kind.' Does that sound better?"

Adelene frowned. "I'm just protecting him. They don't understand him."

"He's a robot."

"Yes, but he—he—"

"He what?"

"He has emotions."

"Oh," Sara said with sarcastic attentiveness, raising her chin, "The robot has a mind of its own now."

"Could you stop joking around about this? I'm being serious."

"No, no, no, Adelene. You've got it all backwards. *You're* the one who's kidding around. *I'm* the one who's being serious. You have no idea what you're dealing with here."

"What do you mean?" Adelene asked, a slight frown forming above her eyes. She hated it when Sara looked at her with that despondent frustration in her eyes, as if Adelene completely sidestepped reality.

"You don't have a *clue*, do you? You don't even *understand* why They really want him back, do you?"

For a moment Adelene seemed about to speak, but her lips tightened and she gave no response.

Sara sighed in exasperation. "Why do you suppose is it so much more *criminal* to shelter a robot from the Laboratories than it is to steal an apple from the hydroponic farms or—or to set an activated kindergarten Teacher on fire with a laser beam?"

"But I'm not a criminal!"

"Oh but trust me, to *Them* you are. And you're menacing too. I bet the Onweald cries Himself to sleep every night"—she bent over the trashcan and spit out her chewing gum—"thinking of what to do to find this Olio of yours."

"Sara, what are you talking about?"

"I'm just saying that the android you've got with you, They've got it out of their reach and its bothering Them now—and I can tell you there's a good enough reason for that. How did he say he opened that coded door before you almost got Detained?"

"He didn't. But he'd been coming more than once. He figured it out."

"So you're saying its *normal* that after a few weeks of going back and forth from here to there he had just *figured* it out—a confidential access key installed by the *Authorities*? Adelene, you just don't get it! A versatile robot from one of the Labs in the g-Negative zone isn't just a pile of shiny composite buzzing around and saying random shit all day. It's a big, fat, Hard Drive of information—that's what it is. Everything you could possibly want to know about the *Inceptum Fidelis* is stored somewhere right in that little guy's mind."

"*Everything?*"

"What—You wanna bet? It's why They're after him, that's for sure." She grabbed rubber band lying on the desk and stretched it between her fingers. "You come up with a better explanation for all this mayhem centered around getting the little bugger back, let me know." She closed an eye and squinted, aiming the rubber band at the Teacher's inert body. Her eyes followed it as it shot across the room and bounced off with a clank. "Oh!" She exclaimed, sinking down into the chair again with a loutish smile, "Did you see that? Right in the eye!"

Adelene ignored her. She stared down at the floor, and then across the room to where the Teacher lay with its head drooping down like that of an old marionette. The light of day reflected off the Teacher's rigid, translucent limbs. It was almost noon. Finally she said in a shriveled voice, "What do want me to do then?"

"Oh, I don't want you to do anything. Just to keep him nice and safe wherever it is you keep him. Once you find him, of course."

"But you said it was criminal to—"

"Adelene, just listen to me. See, whatever *They* need, we need. So we need him—bad."

"What do you mean, 'we need him'? Whose 'we'? Sara, what are you talking about?"

"Don't you understand? I'm talking about you, me, Hacker, *everyone!* We could have access to all the information, all the secrets, all the passcodes in the world! Imagine what this could mean!"

"Sara, if what I told you gave you any ideas about rebelling or escaping, I want you to know that I won't be part of any of it! It's harder than you think. Just forget it all. It's better that way."

Sara heaved herself out of the chair and, finding her way around the desk, she took a few steps closer to Adelene, tilting her head slightly to one side, her hazel eyes fixed onto her. "You know," she said, and unless—as one might think—it was simply the glow of the dim ceiling light that gave the illusion, there was a flame in the girl's eyes when she spoke again, "What people don't seem to accept is that the Authorities are hiding things from us."

"Sara!" Adelene screeched, her eyes wide with alarm. "Are you crazy? Mind what you say!"

"Just listen to me! We're all being manipulated into thinking that our Society is *normal*—just like it is on Earth—and that the way it is run is honorable and perfectly virtuous, but if we all just opened our eyes and *looked around* and became aware of the veil the Authorities have slowly place on our eyes we'd understand that this is *not*—"

Adelene dashed towards Sara and pressed her hand against the girl's mouth. "That's enough, Sara! You'll get us both Detained!"

Sara tore Adelene's hand away. "What do *I* care whether or not I get Detained! Does *anyone* in this world even *know* what it means to be 'Detained'? Does it mean 'jailed,' or 'demoted,' or does it mean '*killed*'? *I'd* like to know!"

"Well, you shouldn't! The government's business is not ours!"

"That's what everyone told you when you were little, isn't it? That's what the Nurses told you, and the Teachers, too. *The will of his Excellency the Onweald, All-seeing and All-powerful, is irrefutable in its loyalty to justice, and must be adhered for the greater good, for peace, and for order and stability throughout our thirty states and its populace of three-hundred-thousand on the destined journey towards a New Beginning for mankind.* It's what we are all told. And why do you believe it? Because you're scared. You're scared not to believe Them. You're scared to go against Them, and that's exactly what They want to provoke. They tighten their grip through fear, and that way His power is greater. That's why They're all poison—the Teachers, the Nurses, the Droids, the Admirals—*All* of Them."

"You have no right to think that way! You speak like an Askancist, Sara! You're out of your mind, you don't know what you're saying and you're frightening me!"

For a moment Sara said nothing. She shook her head slowly, her eyes dark. She answered with a low voice. "I'm not the one frightening you, Adelene."

There suddenly came a crashing sound from somewhere in the dark hallway outside the open door. Sara dropped down onto the cold floor without a sound, pulling Adelene down with her. Both girls crouched behind the desk, motionless. Adelene could feel her heart pounding loudly in her chest.

There was a faint clamor down the hallway and the same strange speech sounded, as broken as if it came from a voice receiver. *"87327,"* the voices said, *"Capture... Operation Z9X0..."* Then, just as suddenly as they had started, the noises ceased.

"We need to get out of here," Sara whispered, "This place isn't safe anymore. Come with me." She rose, pulling Adelene along with her, and tiptoed to one of the windows. She bit her lip as she forced it open. The stagnant air of the room mingled with the fresh breeze that swarmed in from the open window.

"I can't believe They don't have alarms down here," Adelene remarked.

Sara pushed her through the open window and said, "Maybe They *do* and it just takes time for it to turn *on.*

Hurry up."

The two girls stumbled out into the flowering gardens and scurried quietly and warily into the dense trees gathered further down.

"Where do we go to now?" Adelene stammered, out of breath.

"Remember that place I told you about? The old barn in the Twenty-First? That's our new meeting place now. I don't see anywhere safer."

Adelene nodded and looked up at the treetops. "Do you think there could be microbots in the trees?

"Let's hope not," Sara answered, walking further into the woods. "We need to find someway out of Middeton from here, and then we'll go down into the Metro and take whatever public transportation we can find."

"You sure we shouldn't take private? It's safer to be alone in a car than with all those people."

"Yeah, but you find yourself face-to-face with one of Them."

"You really think the Drivers would be aware of this kind of thing?"

"Who knows? Honestly, I trust what that old lady told you about not going down into the transportation Complex that one night. I mean, did you even think the *Teachers* would be aware? I didn't. And they are."

"O.K, O.K, fine. We'll take public."

"Which way's the northern outlet?"

"I'm not sure."

"You don't know your way around your own division?"

"Yes I do! I just don't often go wondering in the forests behind buildings that much! Especially when it's this close to the West Wall."

"Why? Does the Wall scare you?"

"I'm not scared of the Wall. It just makes me... uneasy."

Sara pushed a tree branch out of her way. "Yeah. Well, I

guess you can put it that way too," she said.

16 CENTRUM SOLIS

In one hand the man held his violin, and in the other he held a long brown violin bow. The man was tall and well built. He wore a blue vest with a high collar and a small white scarf tucked into it, and he held himself elegantly. He stood where the straight path ended, in front of two large doors behind which he could see a vast, illuminated room. Inside, a wide staircase spiraled upwards. The man was nervous. The doors of the white palace opened slowly, majestically, and the man entered. The walls coughed with the echo of his footsteps. The floor was so smoothly polished that he could see his reflection sinking beneath his feet. Marble columns stretched up to the ceiling, adorned at their extremities with detailed sculptures of eagles, snakes and lean figures dancing. The ceiling itself was a domed fresco, and the walls were checked with paintings of the Onweald, and of his leopard, and of pretty women with exotic birds in their arms. The intimidating beauty of the place forced the man to slow his pace. Suddenly, an android came to block his way and asked him for his name.

"My name is Brynn Wells," said the man.

"Wells," The android echoed, its eyes fixed onto him.

"That is correct."

"You are not expected here. Where are you from?" There was a spiral nebula drawn in one of the android's eyes. It was the well-known symbol of the Centrum Solis and it made the man anxious.

"I am from Bainsbridge."

"What Division is Bainbridge?"

"The Nineth, sir."

"Do you come alone?"

"Yes, sir."

"Who is this?" the android asked, pointing at the violin.

"This is my musical instrument, sir."

"Please deactivate it now."

"It isn't Intelligent."

"I see," the android said, studying the violin with the laser scanner in its eyes. "How old are you and how much do you weigh?"

"Oh—well, I—I don't see how such information is relevant," the man answered, taken aback.

The android paused. "Are you male or female?"

It was always an odd question to receive, but after all, the interrogator was a robot and could not easily tell the difference. "I am male," he answered.

There was another pause, and the android suddenly seemed irritated. "Then why are you here?" it asked.

"I am here to play for His Excellency the Onweald. I seek Recognition." The man's voice echoed across the high ceiling.

"Recognition," repeated the android in a placid voice. It turned around, and began to ascend the stairs without another word. It did not ask the man to follow, but the man followed anyway.

At the top of the stairs they crossed two fair-skinned young women in florid white dresses, their hair embellished with golden beads and diamonds. Both of them had soft green eyes. Hanging from a thin gold chain around their necks was a pendant of pure gold, shaped into a spiral nebula. Upon seeing him they looked down at their feet and hurried silently down the steps, holding one another's hands. The man followed them with his eyes until they had vanished. When he turned his head back around, the android was gazing at him. The man felt a cold chill run up his back. They walked on. The android led him down a wide hallway arrayed with more sculptures and paintings, and past the tall doors at its end.

The Onweald was sitting in a high, upholstered chair, with one elbow planted in the velvety side support, and his strong jaw reposing on his fist. He was not a very tall man. In fact, he was rather short. The leopard lay next to him, resting with its paws crossed under its spotted head. The man suppressed his astonishment and gave a quick bow, but the Onweald paid him no attention. There was a woman dancing to peaceful music in front of the Onweald. She was lean and light-footed. She had beads in her long, wavy hair that undulated gracefully with every motion she made accompanying the music. She was very beautiful, the man thought. He tried to find the source of the splendid music, but it seemed to come from everywhere at once. The room itself was singing.

The music felt the way it did when the man played his violin by himself, sitting on a rock in a lonely meadow by the waterfalls of Bainbridge, and the music would envelope him, take over his senses and plunge him into a world of sound. The meadow danced and the breeze danced and the world seemed to suddenly stretch far beyond the Walls. It was as if he were the sun and the music were his rays of light, flowing infinitely from his core into boundless space. The man's hand tightened around his violin and he took a deep breath. It made him nervous to hear such beautiful music.

Finally, the woman finished her dance and the music ceased.

"Splendid," the Onweald said clapping his hands. The corners of his lips were turned slightly upwards into a smile. He turned his attention to the man. "Ah, the musician!" he exclaimed welcomingly, "Am I right?"

The man bowed. "My name is Brynn Wells, Your Excellency. I am a violinist."

"Yes, indeed. Welcome to my abode," the Onweald said, raising his arms up by his sides with a proud smile in his eyes, as if he were lifting the entire Centrum Solis in his hands. He did not rise from his chair. "From where do you come to seek Recognition in my presence?"

"Bainbridge," the man answered. "The Nineth Division, my Onweald."

"Ah, yes, Bainbridge. I adore that little town."

"I find it rather quiet."

"Quiet, but very beautiful!" The Onweald turned to the android. "Servant, wine," he ordered, waving his arm at the slender figure, as if he were shooing away a bothersome fly.

"Please, my Onweald, do not bother. I am not thirsty."

"Ah, I insist. A little wine will do both of us good. You are my guest, and I take much pleasure in the proper treatment of my guests. Away with you, Servant."

The Servant left, and the violinist followed it with his eyes, full of apprehension, because the young dancer was gone too, and he was left alone with the Onweald. The leopard was asleep at its master's feet.

There was an uncomfortable silence, and the Onweald did nothing to break it. He did not address one word to the man. He looked out the great windows lined across the wall of the room that faced the garden. The man looked out as well and was suddenly caught with dizzying incredulity. It was not the Lights that glimmered beyond the windows, and whose soft rays poured gently into the Onweald's palace; It was the setting Sun, and it gleamed onto a beautiful lake that ended far, far across this dreamlike landscape, where high mountains rose into a cloudless sky.

"It is stunning, isn't it?" The Onweald suddenly said. He had seen the man stare.

"Yes—Yes, indeed," the man stammered, instantly pulling his gaze away. "Very beautiful."

"It's an illusion."

The doors opened once more and the Servant walked in to serve the wine. The man thanked the Servant and looked at his wine glass. There was a small diamond laced into the stem. It caught the rays of the sun and gleamed with reflected light. The Centrum Solis, the center of the Sun.

The Onweald turned the glass three times in his fingers before lifting it to his lips. He gulped down the alcohol fervently to the last drop, and said, "Please, drink."

The man took a sip of the wine. A divine savor sunk over his tongue. He had never tasted finer a wine.

"So, you are the famous violinist." The Onweald said, petting the leopard. The creature sat on its haunches, wide-awake now, watching the man with its dark and beastly eyes.

"If you say so, my Onweald." The man said. He looked at the leopard warily.

"Don't mind Ellie, she won't hurt you," the Onweald said, passing a hand between the leopard's ears and across its well groomed, spotted pelt. "Gorgeous animal, isn't she?" The Onweald's smile was placid and unchanging. It came to the man that maybe it wasn't a smile at all.

"Yes, indeed, my Onweald."

"That violin of yours is rather worn down. I can procure you a better one if you wish."

"That is very kind of you, but I play best on this violin."

"You are a composer, am I right?"

"Yes, you Excellency."

"Now, if I like your music, I will appoint you as one of my Musicians. If not, I am afraid you shall need to depart with haste, as I have little time to waste on trivial complications."

The man's eyes lit at the thought of becoming one of the Privileged. Until now, it has seemed an unattainable lifelong dream. "Your Excellency, it would be an honor to—"

"Please, the honor is all mine," the Onweald cut him off, leaning back comfortably in his cushiony chair. "Now, pray begin to play."

The man lifted his violin onto his shoulder and gently touched the strings with the lean brown bow. His eyes wondered out the tall windows again. As the sun set behind the mountains its light floated in the lake like a wave of reddish paint diffusing at the surface. The calls of the white swans reposing on the tranquil water echoed like soft music in the man's ears. He closed his eyes, and then he began to play.

17 SHIVER

The boy looked down at his cricket. The yellowish light of the house carved jagged shadows in the folds of his rich clothing. The snowflakes caught in the cashmere check scarf around his neck had melted into glistening beads of water. He must have been no more than seven or eight years old.

The woman looked at her domestic, then at the boy, and clasped her shawl against her neck. "What's your name?"

The boy's lips moved slightly, but he gave no answer. Behind him, the night howled.

"Here, come inside, it is cold out here." She spoke softly, and made a gesture with her hand, but the boy did not move. "Can you tell us what your name is?" she said once more.

He lowered his chin slightly, just enough for the shadow of the fur hat to shroud his eyes. "I want to stay outside," he finally said.

"Why, dear, you cannot stay out in the cold like this!" Her own words made her shiver.

"*Domina,* please, I need a horse."

She remained silent for a moment, her lips slightly parted

and her eyes frozen, in puzzled contemplation, onto the little boy. "Come," she said, her voice hasty with concern, "Come in, dear. You seem very lost."

The boy stepped back warily. "Will you give me a horse?" he asked.

"Why, what for?"

"We cannot walk. Because it would take to long and it is too cold." His breaths formed warm vapor that dissolved into the frozen wind sweeping across his rosy cheeks.

"Whom do you mean, my child?" she asked.

The boy made no answer.

And then the android stepped forward and said, in a calm, still tone, "My mistress urges you to come inside, little one. It is not reasonable to stay out in the cold. You will be ill." It held out its slender metallic hand.

The boy looked down at the cricket between his hands, then into the domestic's gleaming red eyes. He said nothing.

"He won't leave the bug," the woman muttered.

"I will take the cricket," said the android.

Hesitantly, the boy placed the small black shape into the android's hand. It was stiff and silent, but it moved slightly between Alon's smooth metallic fingers. "His name is Shiver," the boy said. He took the android's hand.

"And what is yours?"

"Lành." In his muddy, snow-covered boots, he stepped over the threshold of the door and into the warm room bathed in gentle light. He looked cagily at the woman as he entered. When he saw that her worried eyes were fixed onto him, he clutched the domestic's hand more firmly.

He was brought to the kitchen and seated at the low wooden table. The fire melted the snow on his clothes and made them humid against his frail body, but the boy refused to take off his scarf or his hat. The woman served him hot cocoa in a demitasse and watched him drink quietly. She gave him knitted gloves to warm his reddened hands but he refused to put them on. Who was this little boy in fancy clothes, timid and alone, who seemed lost and confused? Who was this displaced little one who came from nowhere to her doorstep, who carried a cricket in his hands and called her "domina"? Who was this child who only trusted the android?

"Who is with you, child?" the android asked.

"My sister," he mumbled in the fine, soft wool of his scarf. "And our friends."

"Goodness!" the woman said in a disquieted whisper, covering her mouth with one hand. "How many are you out there?"

The boy did not respond.

"Ask him, Alon," she commanded.

"How many are you?" it reiterated.

"There are nine of us," the boy said softly, "but one is a dog."

"And where are you going like this?"

The boy looked into his empty cup and tucked his cold hands between his knees. "We are looking for help."

18 DIVISION 21

The automated voice over the speakers reverberated in the Transport Station extending in a wide network of vehicles, rails and roads circulating underground. *All passengers of the Local Transportation Automotive must proceed to Interdivisional Metropolitan Complex Level 02. Repeat, all passengers of the LTA must proceed to IMC Level 02, please.*

The headlights of the cars flashed past the station, and then vanished along the polished rails into the tunnels, their lights forming a crescent orb of white that illuminated the walls. Adelene and Sara hurried down the lengthy, worn steps of the staircase leading deeper into the Complex. So far below ground the floor was speckled in spheres of lights, and long stretches of bioLED lights slithered across the ceiling and into the tunnels. The Level 02 platforms were covered in publicity displays whose moving images illuminated the walls in a colorful array of beaming light. Among them, gleaming portraits of the Onweald stared into the station.

The two girls stood along the edge of the platform. There was a ghostly silence.

"Don't say a word to anybody," Sara muttered. The long

train moved quietly out from the tunnel and stopped in front of them. Sara stepped in and Adelene followed. There was no one in the train but a man in a washed leather trench coat and a young woman with a tweed jacket and a white fur hat that hid her eyes when she looked down. Her gloves matched her umbrella. Adelene and Sara sat down on the bench opposite the woman. The train closed its doors and rolled soundlessly through the tunnel.

***

They got out at Anderson University, the Twentieth Division, and borrowed two horses at the local stable. It had been the Architect's idea, when he designed the *Inceptum Fidelis*, to have the horses and the horse-drawn carriages in the villages and towns. Habitants liked the feel of it. Like the cows in the prairies, and the deer, field mice and birds in the forests, the horses reminded them of Earth, and brought calmness and cordiality. These animals were harmless species that did not pose a risk. The rest of the fauna and flora of Earth travelled in the form of frozen seeds, eggs and embryos in suspended animation.

Adelene and Sara saddled their horses and rode down towards the outlet, out of the little town and into the Twenty-First Division. Sand paths led in and out of the woods and across a little bridge, where the pond was speckled in lilies. A soft afternoon radiance emanated from the Lights above and caressed the leaves of the trees. A field of marguerites carpeted the hilly meadow, and a rocky cliff jutted out of the earth against the Wall, amid large boulders between which plants grew in abundance. At the top of one of the hills in the meadow, quite far from the path, was a large assemblage of hawthorn blossoms and whitebeam trees whose many limbs seemed frozen in a graceful dance. Dissimulated among them was a ligneous shed with a low wooden door and a small window. The horses snorted and whinnied.

"That's it, over there," Sara said, unsaddling her horse. She pointed at the shed. "There."

The girls left their horses at the bottom of the hill, attached in the shade of a tree along the path, and made their way up. The wind formed rivers of air in the tall grass and the chirping of crickets sounded like little bells at their feet.

Adelene looked up at the abandoned shed. She wondered how it could have been of use before it became an old shack of rotting wood. The cool air in the shady cluster of trees held a dry smell of earth and fallen leaves. Sara walked up to the door and knocked.

There came the low murmurings of voices from inside, and then the sound of footsteps. Someone looked out the window, but through the broken glass the face looked dusty and fragmented.

Sara heaved an annoyed sigh. "Lily, it's Sara," she said loudly, "Let me in."

The door opened abruptly, just enough for Lily's head to peak through the crack and for an empty soda can to roll out. Adelene stopped the can with her foot. Lily's eyes fell onto Sara and a reassured smile illuminated her face. "Oh, it's you!" she exclaimed, opening the door completely. Lily was a lean, somewhat undernourished girl of seventeen, with dark brown hair in messy short haircut and blond highlights.

"Adelene and I had a bit of an issue back at the school," Sara said, looking behind her shoulder at Adelene, "so we came here instead."

Lily looked at Adelene. "Oh, O.K," she said, her thin eyebrows slightly furrowed in confusion. She stepped to the side and let them come in. On her shoulder sat a tiny grey hamster with long translucent whiskers and a soft white underside, munching on a peanut shell. It was a stocky little creature named Bear, with tiny feet and a small pink nose. Sara didn't like Lily's hamster. *Watch that he doesn't shit on you*, she would say mockingly. *I'm telling you, one day he's gonna catch some unknown disease and kill us all.*

The shed smelled of wood and old fire ash. It was about five meters long and four meters wide, and the only furniture was a tall, dark shelf and a table made of thick, uneven slabs of walnut wood held up by four sturdy aspen branches. On the table were soda cans, a chewed pencil, an empty popcorn bag and a computer. Hacker was slumped down on the chair, facing the fire with his cap over his eyes and dozing with his legs stretched out insouciantly. The fireplace was made of red bricks in the wall on the left of the door, sullied here and there with old clouds of soot.

The wooden shelf stood against the wall opposite the door and seemed to hold nothing but a thick film of dust particles between its timeworn ridges. A boy with dark, curly hair and pale skin sat in the corner, a paper book in his hands and a small jar by his side. There was a reddish, rumpled old mat on the floor in front of it, and Abebi sat on it with her legs crossed, picking at the pieces of rotten wood stuck between the knots of shaggy fabric.

Barely fourteen years old, Abebi Biobaku Olanrejawu, or Beb, was the youngest of the group. She had long, wavy black hair and a cheerful temperament that rarely ever died down. Her mother and three older sisters had left their disease-infected village in South Africa after the death of their father, and their mother had remarried many years later to Abebi's father, whom she had met Sedurm, the city in Saudi Arabia where all future habitants of the Inceptum Fidelis were relocated in the few months before the Departure. Upon seeing Sara and Adelene entering, Abebi's lips parted into a big smile.

"Hey, what's up?" she said.

"Apparently, they're in trouble." Lily answered, walking up to Hacker nonchalantly and slapping him teasingly on the cheek, twice. "Wake up, Hacker. They're here."

Hacker raised his head and opened his eyes with a dazed expression. He looked around and stretched his arms lazily.

Abebi laughed. "Hacker was up all night yesterday," she said, "on the computer. Doesn't even tell us what he's doing, he's so concentrated. All he sayin' is, 'Hold on, hold on, I'm almost done!' He's not going anywhere with that." She let out another laugh.

"Wait and see," Hacker mumbled.

"Hacker, how'd it feel to be the only guy among us ladies?" Lily said teasingly.

"It's like hell," Hacker said in a sleepy voice, pulling his cap back down over his face and leaning back in the chair.

"You're just saying that!" Lily said, "You know you love us!"

"Yeah, he knows he loves us," Beb rejoined, "I can see him smiling under that cap there! That not a frown back there! He can't hide it! Where would you be without us, Hacker?"

The two girls giggled.

Adelene looked at the boy sitting silently in the corner by the shelf. "Who's he?" she asked discretely.

"Oh, that's my neighbor," Abebi answered, "Sylvan Straytop. He's kind of shy." Then she lowered her voice and added, "His parents are divorced and I'm basically his only friend. He rarely ever sees his father, and from what I've heard his mother is recovering from a recurring clinical depression."

"What's he doing here?" Sara asked, barging in with a tone of slight annoyance.

"He followed Beb and I all the way here," Lily rejoined.

"Oh how wonderful, Beb! How about we get all thirty Divisions to come follow us to our secret meeting place?" Her gaze fell onto the withdrawn figure scornfully.

"What's he got there in that jar?" Adelene asked.

"It's a bumblebee," said Abebi. "Sylvan likes insects. He knows what they eat and everything. He's quite the expert with little creatures like that."

Sylvan looked up indifferently. He wasn't particularly handsome. He had hollow cheekbones and small blue eyes lined rather close to his nose. There was a certain oddity to him, indistinct and vague, in his manner of gazing at them, in his flimsy appearance and quiet perplexity.

Adelene smiled warmly. She couldn't tell how old the boy was, but he couldn't be much older than she was.

Lily popped open a soda can and sat down on the mat next to Abebi. "So, tell us everything," she said, looking at Adelene and Sara, who stood in front of her.

They sat down next to one another on the parquet floor, and Sara was the one who began to speak. She explained Adelene's peripeteia in Flemington the week before, how it was a versatile robot named Olio that brought her there, and how she and the robot had now unknowingly become the absolute center of attention for the Authorities. Abebi, Lily and Hacker listened with concerned intensity.

"You see, the minute you told me you owned one of their precious lab robots, I knew you'd get yourself in trouble one way or the other because people usually don't get away with infractions like that," Sara added, turning to Adelene with a deadpan expression.

She tried to hide a teasing smile, but its reflection was etched in her voice, "I just didn't know you'd manage to find the *worse* way of getting yourself in trouble for it."

Adelene looked at her with a hunted look and said nothing. For a moment everyone was silent.

Lily put a hand on Adelene's shoulder and said, "Don't worry, we're here for you. We won't let anything happen to you."

"I say Adelene shows us the way and we steal one of those ships!" Beb exclaimed roguishly, with a quick chortle that soon turned into a wholehearted laugh, as if she knew her proposition to be utterly absurd.

"That might actually be doable," came Hacker's voice. He was still sitting on his chair with the cap over his face as if the Light-rays passing feebly through the dust-stained glass of the window were bothering him.

"I'm not leaving the ship," Adelene said harshly, "I'm not. You weren't there with me that day. Hacker, the Droids were shooting. They were armed and they were shooting at us."

Lily, Abeli and Sara had fallen silent. They watched Hacker lift his cap with one hand to look at Adelene. "I'm not *saying* we're going to do it," he said, "I'm just saying that it's possible to leave the ship."

19 BOOKS

"You're just being unrealistic, Hacker" Adelene snapped. "Just because you're good with computers doesn't mean you'll hack through the whole ship's security system."

"I'm not saying I can—not alone at least. But there are five of us. Six if you count *him.*" Hacker gave a slight shake of the head in Sylvan's direction.

Sara snorted with laughter. "Let's leave it at five," she chuckled.

"Yes, and there are two hundred thousand of Them!" Adelene retorted. "This voyage was planned out for decades. They've had everything marked out and calculated with the greatest accuracy since the beginning. *Androids* built this ship, Hacker. *Androids.* We're not turning back."

"We can try—"

"I don't want to turn back, Hacker."

"Then leave this place, then!" He said harshly. "Why are you even here if you—"

"Because you led me into this!" she snapped, "All of you!"

"No, *you're* the one who led *yourself* into this. Look! Everything that happened there in Flemington was no one's fault but yours. You did all that yourself. You're just like the rest of us, slowly realizing that everything you've been struggling not to believe was in fact the cold, hard truth. You have to decide what you *want*, Adelene. You're either in or out of this. Either you trust us or you trust Them. There's no in-between."

For a moment she was silent, staring into his eyes, her lips quivering as if she were about to cry. "I trust you," she finally said.

He smiled.

"But *please*," she added in all seriousness, "just don't do anything stupid."

In the long silence that followed, they could hear the bee in the jar buzzing frantically, hitting its head repetitively against the glass as if it were strong enough to perforate through the transparent rigidity. Sylvan sat motionless in the corner, with downcast, vacant eyes.

"You should let that bee out, Sylvan," Lily said gently, perturbing the silence.

"My bee is very happy in the jar," Sylvan mumbled, "I give him sugar." And then placed his elbows on his knees and held the book up to his face, as if Lily had disturbed him in his reading.

Adelene stood up and walked up to Sylvan. "I'm Adelene," she said, kindly, a smile reclaiming her soft features. She held out her hand.

Sylvan hesitated, and then he shook hands with her. "My name is Sylvan," he said, "My favorite book is *Soul of Stone*, by Frederick Hinge."

On the mat, Abebi repressed a laugh, but in her eyes it was as obvious as the black-rimmed glasses on her nose. Adelene tried to read the title of the book he was reading, but the Search Engine in her contact lenses could not identify it for her, and she could not get more than a small glimpse of the black lettering on the beige cover. "What are you reading?" she asked.

Sylvan stopped reading and looked at the title.

"JOHN LOCKE
'Treatise Of Civil Government' (1688)."

"Can I see your book?" Adelene asked gently.

"It isn't mine," he said, "I found it on the shelf."

"Oh, O.K. But can I see it for a second?"

Sylvan closed the book and handed it to her.

Sticking out from the yellowed pages was a bookmark. It was a small piece of cellulose paper, wrinkled and dented in so many ways that its corners swooped downwards like lopsided ears. On both sides of the paper, in runny blue ink, were printed a succession of tiny numbers. Adelene stared at the strange bookmark intrusively, but when Sylvan snatched it away, her attention came back to the book itself.

"Whose John Locke?" she asked.

No one answered because nobody knew.

"Can't find anything about him on here," Hacker said as he strolled perplexedly through the search results on his computer.

There were pen marks and side notes scribbled all over the pages. Adelene flipped through them pryingly, and began to read. *"To understand political power aright, and derive it from its original, we must consider what state all men are naturally in, and that is a state of perfect freedom to order their actions and dispose of their possessions and persons as they think fit, without asking leave, or depending on the will of any other man."* She stopped reading and started blankly at the passage. She said nothing.

"What's wrong? What does it say?" Sara asked with curiosity.

Adelene turned the book around in her hands like a relic. "Who is this man?" she mumbled in a barely audible voice.

"Can you read it to us?" Abebi said.

"This book questions the Law."

Sara moved closer. "What did you say?"

"It questions the Law." Adelene skimmed through the pages again and her eyes fell onto a passage titled, *Of Political or Civil Society*. She handed the open book to Sara. "Read it yourself," she said.

Sara took the book and read aloud. "'Hence, it is evident, that absolute monarchy, which by some men is counted the only government in the world, is indeed inconsistent with civil society...'" Her voice trailed off as she frowned in disbelief and read the rest to herself, "*...and so can be no form of civil government at all.*"

"Sara! Don't just read it to yourself! Go on!" Lily said.

The others listened without interrupting. Sylvan, too, sat quietly, watching Sara read. "'For he being supposed to have all,'" she continued, "'both legislative and executive power in himself alone, there is no judge to be found; no appeal lies open to any one who may fairly and indifferently and with authority decide, and from whose decision relief and redress may be expected of any injury or inconveniency'"—she closed the book—"'that may be suffered from or by his orders.' There. I read it."

"Adelene's right," Lily said, "It is a banned book."

"How do *you* know?" Abebi asked, "The Onweald is our pilot, not our monarch. This man isn't talking about *our* government. The year 1688, that's over four-hundred years ago."

Sara leaned over her with a haughty smile on her face. "How much power would you say His Excellency the Onweald has, Beb?"

"A lot of power."

"*Absolute* power," Sara corrected her.

"But he's not a monarch! He has ensured the utmost security and order in our Society for nearly seventeen years."

Sara tapped the book cover. "Maybe, but *this* guy, John Locke, says otherwise. And that's why you'd have to think twice before strolling around the Centrum Solis with this book under your arm."

"Does it say whom it belongs to anywhere?" Lily asked, standing up and walking towards them to peer at the book in Sara's hand.

"Well, it definitely belongs to *someone*," Adelene affirmed. "Look at all these notes on the side of the page."

"Do you see a name anywhere?"

Sara threw a mocking glare over her shoulder. "Lily, why would *anyone* write their name inside a *banned book*?"

Adelene took the book from her and flipped through it. She glanced at one of the few blank pages at the beginning and said, "Who's E.R.?" The initials were scribbled in dark blue ink at the very bottom of the page, so small that she had to squint to decipher the inscription.

"E.R.?"

"Yes. Someone's initials, I guess."

"Well whoever it is isn't afraid of getting Detained."

"Eugenia Robinson!" Hacker called out, still slouching detachedly in the chair.

Sara looked at him scornfully. "Hacker, either you help us out or you just shut up."

"What? You don't know Eugenia Robinson?" Hacker rejoined friskily, putting his headphones on, "The girl from Westerly? She looks like a hardcore Askancist to me." And he laughed.

Sara rolled her eyes up and heaved a sigh.

"Maybe there are more books in here," Lily said. She looked at the shelf ridges one by one, passing her hand blindly across the dusty surface of the higher ones. She rose onto her toes to reach the top shelf. Her hand tore through a succession of old spiderwebs and stopped midway across the wooden board. "Here!" she exclaimed, reaching her other hand in and pulling out a heavy pile of beige-covered paper books. "Look!"

Adelene took one of the books from Lily's pale hands and read the title. "*Candide*, by Voltaire." She shook her head. "I don't know any of these authors!"

"Do you think *all* of these books are banned?" Lily asked, gently wiping the dust off of each cover with her hands.

"Well, whoever the owner is definitely tried to hide them here. The books must have been pretty dear to them."

"This one's in French!" Lily said, flipping through the pages of a book with a torn cover. "Montesquieu, *De l'Esprit des lois.*"

Sara gasped and snatched the book from Lily's hands. "I know who this is!" she exclaimed, staring down at the French text. "I know who this is!"

"Who? *Montesquieu?*"

"No, no, no—I mean I know who 'E.R.' is! Etienne Rhynes! That guy from Jotham! His parents are French."

"Does he go to our school?"

"No, but he used to. He's at John Rhilay University this year, I think. He's eighteen."

"Oh, the cute blond guy with the Labrador?" Lily smirked.

"Yeah, that's him."

"What makes you think he reads these books, though?" Lily peered down at the pile of old, dull-looking books.

"Well, first of all there's nothing Rhynes *doesn't* read. And second of all I've never met anyone else around here who reads old-world paper books in *French* and whose name has the initials E.R."

"Eugenia Robinson!" Hacker yelled out again with a teasing laugh.

"Hacker, shut up and do your work."

The boy snickered and put his headphones back over his ears.

Suddenly Abebi cried out, "The ashes!" and all of the faces turned to her inquiringly.

She was staring into the fireplace, her eyes wide with astonishment. There, lost among the old remnants of the fire, blackened and smeared by the flames, lay a dark mass of withered pages loosely held together in a slumping, ghostlike form. She reached her hand into the ashes and pulled out a small piece of paper. Its edges were burned and wrinkled, and there was writing on its surface. In her hand was a page from a book.

Adelene walked up to her and took the piece of paper from her hand.

"BILL OF RIGHTS (1689)
An Act Declaring the Rights and Liberties of the Subject and
Settling the Succession of the Crown"

That was all that was written on the page. And yet again, in a slightly burned corner of the page, the initials, "E.R." were scribbled in black ink. They were all silent for a while, staring at the ashes. Even Hacker had abandoned his computer and was standing next to them, his eyes focused on the miraculously intact piece of paper rescued, someway or another, from the flames.

"I don't understand," said Lily, in a tone as confused as the soft light seeping through the shattered window. "Why have some of these books been kept hidden and others burned?"

"It makes no sense," Sara added. "You don't just burn your own books like that."

"Maybe he got scared that he'd get caught," Abebi proposed.

"Yeah, but then he would've burned all of them."

Outside, the wind washed over the small barn and howled between the uneven slates of wood that shaped it. It carried with it the peaceful whinnies and neighs of the horses left at the bottom of the hill.

"Guys, look at this!" Hacker suddenly exclaimed. He sat staring at the old computer screen, an incredulous smile illuminating his eyes. "I have something!"

Sylvan Straytop looked up at him from the corner by the shelf with a kind of passive curiosity, then his eyes fell back into his book. The four girls crowded around the tiny wooden table. "What've you got?" Sara asked.

"Some kind of memory-storage website. I bet not even Privileged families can access this stuff. Look at this." He flipped through a series of frozen images materializing onto the screen. They were somewhat grainy and outlandish. Some depicted beautiful landscapes like the ones Crazy Marius painted in the basement of Middleton Church, but these images were more detailed, the depth more defined, the colors more subtle, and the whole not dreamlike but real. There were images of fields of tall grasses through which passed railroads and rivers, others of people walking in the streets of a strange city, with buildings that seemed to stretch as high as the Mountains behind them.

The Mountains. Sara gasped at their overpowering beauty. Her mother's words rang in her head. *There were no Walls on Earth. Only the Sky, and the Mountains.*

These were images of the Earth.

"What is this?" Lily blurted out, struggling to make sense of it all. The screen responded to her words and the image was instantly enlarged until it filled the screen completely, and suddenly it burst to life. A world of sound and vibrancy bloomed in front of their eyes. The people in the image moved and spoke, and behind them automobiles drove by in a bright light that emanated from everywhere at once. The thought struck them like lightning—This radiant brightness was the Sunlight.

Adelene and Abebi pushed their way closer to the screen. Sylvan, too, had finally stood up and come quietly among them, and he stared at it with the same transfixed eyes.

"Is it a film?" Abebi asked, never shifting her gaze from the screen. "An old film from Earth?"

No one answered her. Eyes were fixed on the beauty of the images, on the immensity of the world inside the tiny screen. The people spoke a language that none of them knew. Japanese, maybe. Or Korean.

"I think it's a story," Lily said, "Part of a story, at least. The woman with the short black hair, she keeps reappearing. See?"

The view shifted to a small table in a quiet restaurant, where a young woman sat with her legs crossed and her eyes wondering out the window, waiting for someone. A waiter came up to her and refilled her cup of tea. The woman gave a polite smile.

"She's very pretty," Abebi remarked evasively. There was a hint of caginess in her voice, as if the words conflicted with another thought that troubled her—that troubled all of them. The woman in the screen was radiant with beauty, her smile polite and happy. Her world seemed so peaceful, and vast, and different. Was this the war-torn, poverty-ridden, polluted and unstable Earth they learned about in school?

A tall man in a simple shirt and tie walked into the restaurant and sat in front of the woman. He kissed her hand and said something that made her blush.

"That must be her husband," Adelene said.

"No," Lily said, squinting her eyes as she tried to make sense of the dialogue. "I think they're just friends, and he's in love with her."

Suddenly the screen went dark. The restaurant and the man and the woman and the Sunlight all vanished.

"What happened?" Sara snarled, "Hacker, what happened? What did you do? You touched something!"

"I didn't do anything," Hacker said defensively, lifting both hands away from the computer. The small green letters flickered across the screen in irregular spasms: *Record Incomplete or Missing.*

Groans of disappointment left their mouths.

"Well, let's watch another one!" Abebi rejoined cheerfully.

"Hopefully some of these films are saved in full," Hacker said, selecting a new image among a myriad of others.

This time a calm blueness filled the screen—a glistening, undulating body of water. It stretched far into the distance, with nothing but the horizon line splitting it from the endless Sky. A cold shiver ran through Adelene as the camera lens rolled across the gigantic, salty mass of bubbly waves just as dolphins leaped into the air—glimmering grey bodies bursting with energy—and plunged back into the cerulean waters. She took a step back, struggling to take in the gleaming immensity that seemed to strange and yet so familiar. The Ocean.

It was her voice that broke the silence. "I've seen this before."

The eyes that had until now been fixed onto the screen fell onto her.

"What do you mean you've seen this before?" Sara said.

Hacker chortled, "In her dreams, maybe."

"No—I can't remember where—I saw it. The ocean—" Her father's face flashed across her vision and with it a stinging flow of emotions. Dead. Gone. Ocean. Memories. The world seemed to spin, and she grasped the edge of the wooden table for support. "I remember—something—It's so weird. The sensation."

"*Déjà-vu*," Sara grumbled under her breath.

Lily threw her a reproving glare and took Adelene gently by the arm. "You O.K?"

"Yeah, I'm fine," she answered, touching her hand to her forehead. "Just a little tired. I saw my father for a second. He just—flashed across my mind. I don't know why."

Then Hacker gave a disheartened groan and slammed his hand against the table. "Happened again!" he exclaimed, staring at the screen. It was black again. *Record Incomplete or Missing*. "What's the point of keeping all these files if they're damaged?"

"It's a security system." Sylvan's voice came just as unexpectedly, indifferent and withdrawn, as somber as his narrow eyes.

"What? How do you know, Bee-man?" Hacker said, furrowing his eyebrows, the corners of his lips hardly repressing a mocking smile. Sara guffawed.

"It needs to recognize your genetic code to operate correctly," Sylvan continued, "It must have realized you were an intruder in the System. Only the Authorities can access the records without an I.G.C." The boy took his jar in one hand and placed his book carefully back on the shelf. "And don't call me Bee-man. I don't like it." Without another word, he walked out the door and down the steep slope of the hill, disappearing among the trees before any of them could call him back.

20 COPPER

When Etienne was little, his father had told him how the object around his wrist worked. The intricate automatic mechanism behind the two hands that spun endlessly around the circular center, ticking faintly when he placed his ear to it, fascinated him.

"What time is it, Papa?" He would always ask. His father would let out an affectionate laugh under his moustache, and show him the spinning hands. Etienne always knew what time it was—everyone always knew—because it was written everywhere, but his father's watch captivated him just as all of the other objects from Earth did. Looking at the hands was like peering into another world, into the life of the man in his workshop who had handcrafted the little object meticulously, slowly, a long, long time ago.

His father had a camera, too—a digital camera that still worked, although there was no way of saving the pictures—and a compact disk player with an old music album. When he turned ten his father gave them to him. He kept them in his room on the shelf, or on his bedside table, and Jexter never took them away.

But some things he kept secret. He had a copper coin.

One cent, it read, dated *2005*. It wasn't his. He had stolen it from another boy at school when he was in Second Grade. He didn't know where the boy had found it. He didn't know its value, but to him it was a treasure—a secret from Earth. He made up a story for it: He dreamt about where it came from, who it had belonged to, where it had travelled. He wondered who the man was, whose profile was printed on one side of the coin. He must have been important. Like the Onweald.

On the other side were the Latin words *E pluribus, unum*. When he had asked Jexter what it meant, the android's eyes had reddened and he had responded in a harsh voice, "Where did you hear such words, little Etienne?"

"A boy at school," Etienne had answered, frightened.

"What is that boy's name?"

"Liam."

Jexter never answered his question, but the android's unexpected angriness triggered an insatiable curiosity. Etienne hid the copper coin away and never told anyone about it. As a child, he was careful never to touch it again, because after he touched it his fingers had a strange, acrid smell, the smell of blood—the smell of fear. And yet it was that same acrid strangeness that he would later look for in the old crumbling pages of books, or in the deafening sounds of old Metallica CDs, collected and treasured in a secret act of sedition.

21 NOON AND BEE-MAN

The Population Genetics Teacher was a well-designed android with light streaks of purple lining its shiny composite limbs. Probably the latest model. It watched her with cold, threatening eyes that made her heart sink to her stomach. "What is the Founder Effect, Miss Adelene?"

"It is the loss of genetic variation when a very small number of individuals establishes a new population from a much larger population." Her voice was tense. She hated being called on.

"Good. And why is it necessary for us to have an understanding of this?"

"Because our founding population on the ship had to be precisely decided, and chosen from a variety of ethnicities in order to diversify the gene pool as much as possible."

"And what is our population?"

"Three hundred thousand."

"Good. Try not to look down at your notes next time."

The day dragged on like all other school days, from one polished classroom to another. Between lessons, the noisy voices of the students rang in the hallways. At noon, the savory scent of lamb stew and warm bread, duck pâté and fine spices, plum cakes and raspberry cream pies would escape across the tall doors of the Canteen.

When Emmeline was still here, she and Adelene would sit together everyday in the Canteen, always at the same table, by the high windows facing the gardens. They would talk and share laughs for so long that they would almost forget to eat. Then Sara would come by with Hacker halfway through the lunch hour, crash down into a chair next to Adelene and ask them what was for lunch because she was starving. Then Abebi and Lily would come too, and a couple of Hacker's friends would squeeze in as well, until finally there was too much chattering for anyone to hear each other.

Lunchtime was different without Emmeline. A group of younger students sat at Emmeline's table now, and it was harder to find a place to sit. Adelene's eyes swept across the wide room, looking for Sara, and fell onto a lonely table near the wall. She remembered vaguely a tall boy sitting there by himself the year before. Short blond hair and dark blue eyes. Lean figure and mysterious disposition. She knew his name because the girls at her table always prattled on about him, their cheeks flushed, their hands slightly hiding their beaming smiles. Etienne Rhynes. For a whole year she had mistaken him to be Sara's brother, until she noticed the two of them never talked once.

Except that now it wasn't Etienne sitting at the lonely table anymore. It was Bee-man. Sylvan Straytop ate his lunch silently, looking at her from across the room. She smiled kindly, and without hesitating came to sit in front of him.

"Hi," she said.

"Hi, Adelene," he said quietly, his eyes plunged in his lamb stew.

"You're lucky you got the stew. I came in too late and now all they have left is the fish." She gave a small laughed.

Sylvan looked at her plate and chuckled slightly. "But it's Mahi Mahi. It's good. It's my favorite type of fish."

Adelene smiled. "I guess I'll try it then." She took a bite of the moist flakes of tender white meat.

"It's good, right?"

Adelene nodded. It had a salty, sweet taste, but it sickened her to think that it had been synthesized in the Laboratories.

"I love fish. My father says I'll have some for my birthday."

"That's nice. You're lucky. My Familiar makes nothing but carrot broth."

Sylvan laughed, then went back to his plate. It was hard to break the silence after that, but the Canteen was noisy enough to hide the discomfort. Why was she sitting with him anyway? Was it that she felt bad for him, all by himself at his corner table? Or was it out of curiosity for the boy who knew about a Secondary Security System in the Governmental Records?

"When's your birthday?" she asked.

"Tomorrow. My family has organized a celebration. Abebi is coming. You want to come too?"

Adelene was taken aback. "Sure!" she said with a warm smile before her reluctance could manifest itself. Abebi claimed to be Sylvan's only friend. If this was indeed true, then who else could possibly be invited? At least Abebi would be there. Maybe the two of them could joke about it later. "I'll need your address," she added, "Do you live in Middleton?"

He shook his head. "It's not at my house. It's at my father's house. It's a little far. I'll come pick you up."

"Oh, thank you," she said, a little puzzled. "That's very kind of you."

There were no personal vehicles above ground. Only horses and bikes. The horses had been the Architect's idea.

He had designed the Ship in a botanical mindset, bent on honoring a harmony between nature and technology. The Onweald would, once in a while, parade in the streets in a slow carriage, saluting the habitants who leaned out from their windowsills waving flags or colorful tissues, smiling at him, hailing him, carrying babies on their shoulders. Perhaps on certain hot days there were bike-taxis carrying Privileged women and their pets and colorful sunshades. In Adelpha or Tammerlaine, on the periphery of the golden gates of the Centrum Solis, a few carriages could be found parked in the Square, awaiting the arrival of an Officer. All other modes of transportation between divisions—trains, automobiles, cargo wagons and other high-speed vehicles—lay confined underground in the network of tunnels and rails below their feet.

They ate in silence. Soon, the Anthem would play its grey tune in every room of the school, a faithful announcement that it was now Noon of the Six Thousand Three Hundred and Fourteenth Day of the Great Voyage of the *Inceptum Fidelis*.

22 INVITED

"He invited you, too?" Abebi exclaimed. They walked side by side along the small gravel path that lined a wooden enclosure, behind which the horses grazed in silence. A small hill sloped downwards on their right, dotted with small blue flowers. The first houses of Middleton lay peacefully at its foot. A light breeze rustled the leaves and a thin veil of clouds masked the Lights.

"Yeah. He did." Adelene tucked her hands in the rough-textured pockets of her trench coat. "Are you going?"

"I don't know," Abebi shrugged. "I'd feel terrible if I didn't, and now that I know you're invited too, I might as well go."

"Do you know where he lives? He said he'd come pick me up, but I don't understand what he means. Is he a Privileged?"

"Not just that," Abebi said with a smile, "I think his father lives in the Sixteenth Division."

"The Sixteenth?" Adelene exclaimed, stopping abruptly.

"Yes, the Sixteenth."

Adelene stared at her incredulously. "Sylvan's father has his own headquarters in the Centrum Solis?"

"I'm not sure, but I did see the mark in his Familiar's eye."

"A spiral nebula?"

Abebi nodded.

"That doesn't mean much. *All* Privileged families have marked Familiars."

Abebi shook her head. "No, only those of high-ranking officials. Look at Mary Clovestone's Familiar, that old pile of metal called Dyllus. He doesn't have the mark—his eye-lenses are barely even functional—but you can't say the Clovestones are just regular habitants. They get seats at the *Charlottina* in Flemington every Sunday evening, and they're driven there in a personal vehicle."

"So you're saying that's where we're going tonight? The Sixteenth Division?"

Abebi smiled enthusiastically. "I'm saying you'd better wear something nice!" She laughed and took Adelene's hand. The two girls tumbled down the slope and made their way back to the village just as a light rain began to fall. They walked across the small square where a couple of children chased one another, their foulards tucked neatly into the collar of their coats.

It was warm inside the house and Myrna bent over the stove with a plate of bread. Abebi saluted her politely. "My respect, *Praeministra.*"

"Myrna, will you do our hair tonight?" Adelene asked enthusiastically.

Myrna smiled, her eyes slightly pausing on Abebi's face. "Of course, Miss Adelene. I would gladly do so."

"Abebi and I are invited to a celebration this evening, at the Centrum Solis!"

"We might get to meet the Onweald in person!" Abebi said, struggling to keep her voice composed and civil under the gust of enthusiasm.

"Oh, heavens!" the android said with a start. "In that case, we must take care to dress you suitably as well." The android sat the two girls on low stools in front of the mirror in the lavatory. As she passed a sturdy brush through Adelene's wet, tangled hair, she continued, "Refinement, order and elegance are virtues that His Excellency values most notably. In His presence, you must look—and act—absolutely flawless. If there is one thing that the Great Voyage must not let you forget, it is the honor and beauty of the human race. You are here to improve and polish humanity, regardless of the ways in which its morality and virtue has been degraded and fouled on Earth. Now, remember your manners. Address every man and woman as *domine* and *domina*, and do not look into the eyes of the Servants when you bow. Do exactly as the Authorities and the bureaucrats tell you."

Adelene beamed with joy. "Do you really think we will meet Him, Myrna?"

"Well, in all likelihood, if the Sixteenth is in effect the lieu of this event, you shall indeed have that honor, Miss Adelene."

The carriage pulled up in front of the small path among the cherry trees. From the behind the tall glass wall that lined the living room the girls watched the Driver curb the horses to a stop.

Adelene glanced back at Myrna. "Is this our transport?"

"Yes," the android answered, "and the Driver signals that you come forward. Head along, then."

Adelene adjusted the folds of her dress before rushing out the door followed by Abebi. It was a beautiful carriage with a sleek duralumin roof and large spoked wheels. Adelene could see her shadowy reflection running along the smooth white fiberglass structure. The Driver's bright purple eyes fell onto them and they immediately composed themselves.

"Adelene Harlow?" The cold voice asked.

"My respect," Adelene said with a slight bow of the head.

"And you are...?"

"Abebi Olanrejawu," Beb replied.

"She's invited, too." Adelene added, her voice tense.

The Driver stared back at her. "Indeed," hissed the mechanical voice. The door of the carriage opened quietly, and two translucent steps materialized like floating magnets in front of it. The Driver motioned them to step on, and the door closed gently behind them. Inside were carbon-fiber bucket seats with bronzed leather covers, softened with plush silk cushions. They looked out the small windows on either side of the carriage, through which the gentle evening light stroked their eager faces.

"We're the luckiest girls alive, you know that?" Abebi chuckled. The carriage began to advance with the rhythmic trotting of the horses.

The trip felt long. Once in a while the horses whinnied, a dog barked, a light breeze rustled the leaves in the trees. The road turned to light gravel, then sand, then cobblestones. It narrowed and widened, straitened and curved repetitively. Adelene counted the outlets as they rode through them one-by-one. A great shadow would suddenly be cast over them—the frontier between two divisions—and Adelene counted. *Twenty-Five.* The horses trotted on.

Village after village, town after town, they all looked the same, but she new all of their names. *Twenty-Four. Twenty-Three.* Lavemore. Delton. Anderson University. When the carriage passed through the Twenty-First Division, she looked closely towards the hill where the wooden shed lay, afraid for a moment that it may be noticeable, but it was well dissimulated among the trees.

Twenty. The small hamlet of Oswin. Another hour passed before they reached Tammerlaine, and crossed into the Seventeenth Division beyond. Like the Twenty-First, the Seventeenth was uninhabited, traversed only by herds of deer and flocks of wild birds. There were few cattle, too, enclosed in wide stretches of wooden fences close to the southern outlet. The Onweald did not like to feel too proximate to the bustle of common towns and villages, and preferred that his own Division be surrounded by woodland.

The horses slowed as they approached the tall golden gates and its six Guards. In the center, a spiral nebula shone like a diamond. The Mark, the Emblem of His power. Slowly, the gates opened.

23 EMERALD EYES

It was a beautiful ballroom, its ceiling adorned with elaborate paintings and arches of gold. Tall windows stretched along the flawless stone walls, illuminating the long buffet table an its thousands of aromatic foods. Adelene walked discretely among the crowd of floridly-dressed men and women, holding Abebi's hand, looking for Sylvan. She caught a glimpse of him speaking to a red-haired man with a stiff countenance.

"Adelene, look!" Abebi exclaimed, freeing her hand, "Plum cakes!"

"Wait—"

"Wait? No, I'm getting a plum cake even if it means pushing aside a few Privileged folk."

"I know, but that man over there—"

"Look, if I'm invited to their party, I might as well act like one of them!" She giggled.

"Beb, that man—I think I know him."

Abebi was gone before she could hear. She hopped eagerly to a silver platter at the buffet tablet, smiling at everyone she crossed. Adelene sighed nervously and pushed her way quietly to where she had seen Sylvan and the red-haired man. The boy was dressed in an elegant high-collared suit, and his hair was neatly held down with gel. He looked older in that outfit. The man with the red hair was similarly dressed, but wore a long, green wool coat. Elegant black trousers fell to the heels of his polished shoes. His eyes were of an evasive, almost translucent blue.

"Ah," he said when he saw her approach, "Who have we here?"

"This is my friend, Adelene." Sylvan smiled. "She came here from Middleton. Adelene, this is my father."

"General Ryffrith," She said with a polite bow. "I think we met before. You knew my father."

The man hesitated, then smiled coldly. "Ah, yes. Miss Harlow, is it? Ace's child."

"Yes, *Domine*."

"Your father was a good man, Miss Harlow. A great friend." He sighed. "What a shame that he is no longer with us." The pallid eyes, in their poisonous hue, stared flatly into hers. "He was a simple engineer, and yet His Excellency the Onweald trusted him almost as much as he trusted me, his Advisor. In fact, if His Excellency were present this night, he would no doubt say a word or to about him. Unfortunately, His Excellency is away. Sylvan, do you know that your friend's father designed, tested and improved the CX79 Automaton? It is a versatile robot used to store information, replicate human learning abilities, and study memory. To date, I presume there are about three hundred such creatures in operation in the Laboratories."

Olio. He meant Olio. Adelene responded with a slight smile, swallowing her apprehension. Her hands were shaky and her face tense. How much did this man know? How much could he know?

The General continued, "I must say such an achievement is worth Recognition. Surly your family has been granted Recognition, Miss Harlow?"

Adelene shook her head slightly. "No, Domine."

"Indeed?" The man's eyebrows rose as though in surprise, forming blunt wrinkles below the curly red hair. "Indeed, how strange. Perhaps..." he paused. "Perhaps the lack of an elaborate and precise tracking system on those little humanoids may have appeared, in the eyes of the Onweald, a significant flaw." His lips tightened into a faint, cruel smile. His eyes, those two poisonous blue darts, stared straight into hers.

"I don't—I don't know." Her voice quivered as she spoke. She didn't like the man. She hated him. She wanted to turn around and disappear into the crowd again, but her feet felt glued to the floor.

"Well, if his experimentations did have such a flaw, I must say, it is a shame none of us has your father's talent to correct it."

Suddenly, Abebi materialized from the mass of colorful robes and hats and grabbed Adelene's arm. "There you are!" In her hand she held a plate with a small white cake in the middle, and handed it to her. "I saved this for you! The coconut truffles disappear as soon as They bring them!" Her eyes fell onto Sylvan and she gave a delighted little cry. "Happy birthday, Sylvan!"

The boy smiled, and mumbled a thank you.

Abebi glanced back at Adelene, then at Ryffrith. "Excuse us," she said, a happy smile still anchored in her face as she pulled Adelene away from them. The crowd absorbed the two of them—a blast of perfumes, rough-textured clothes, music, voices, laughter—until they reached a beautiful white staircase that spiraled up to a second floor, where they could see small groups of guests chatting together. They found themselves standing near a tall fireplace away from the bulk of the crowd. Abebi's beaming smile disappeared and her dark eyes seemed wide with concern. The change came as suddenly as if she had lifted a mask from her face.

"What's wrong?" Adelene asked.

"You won't believe me if I tell you," she whispered, "but I have to tell you." Then her eyes darted frantically in all directions, as if mortified at the thought of being overheard.

"Abebi, what is it?"

"I was standing here—I was looking for you and thought you had gone upstairs—and I saw a group of girls peering in from one of the hallways that branch off the second floor. They all wore long white dresses and they all had blond hair, and the same diamonds around their necks." She covered her face with her hands.

"They're just guests, Abebi, calm down."

"No, you don't understand." She swallowed hard. Her eyes seemed to glisten in the light of the fire, as though with tears. "One of them was—"

"Hey, you two!" said a sudden harsh voice not far from them. Abebi jumped, and Adelene felt her heart sink to her stomach. It was a Servant, walking along the stone wall on their right. "You shouldn't be here!" He wasn't looking at them, but past them, at the mouth of a narrow hallway behind the white staircase. There stood two young women dressed in silky white dresses, their blond hair tied in loose buns. A veil of fear and sadness shrouded the emerald green of their eyes. Around each of their necks hung a golden spiral nebula.

At the servant's words, they gasped and stepped back into the shadows of the hallway. One of the girls lingered a bit longer, ignoring the other, who tugged at the silk sleeve of her dress, and for a second her eyes met Adelene. In that second, a spark of recognition held their gazes together. Adelene's eyes widened in disbelief, and her lips quivered, but no words came out. The whole world seemed to spin around her. The blond hair, the innocent green eyes, the fair skin.

It was Emmeline.

The girl stared back at her one more time, then disappeared into the obscurity. "No! Wait!" Adelene called out. Without thinking, she tried to run towards the entrance of the hallway, but Abebi held her back and the Servant blocked her path. "Please, sir, let me through!"

"I'm sorry, Miss, but guests are not allowed in these headquarters."

"But I know her! I know that girl!"

"That's impossible, Miss. You must be mistaken."

"No, we both know her! Beb, you know her too! It's Emmeline!"

Abebi stood anchored in place, eyes wide with fear. She shook her head, and said nothing.

"Let me direct you back to the main hall," the android said. Adelene felt the Servant's strong metallic hand wrap around her arm. She wrung it free, but it was no use resisting. He pushed the two of them slowly back among the unsuspecting guests. A few had turned their faces towards the commotion, then turned away again, some slightly annoyed, others simply disinterested. Adelene could hear Abebi's faint voice calling her name. The mindless chattering of voices, the stuffy smell of cakes and perfume, all had captured her again. She wanted to disappear from this place and run—run far away—forever. The crowd suddenly felt overwhelming, threatening, suffocating. There is nowhere to run to. There are walls, walls everywhere. The world is full of walls.

She felt another hand on her shoulder and turned around with a gasp. It was a tall man in a grey suit, with a black moustache and tiny eyes staring at her from an oblong face. "Miss Harlow? Please follow me. We shall escort you home safely."

"*Domine*, please, listen to me," she begged him, "Those

girls over there—"

"Please come along, Miss. There is a carriage right outside for you."

"But—"

"Do not worry. All is in order and you shall be home shortly." The man took her arm, and she walked without resisting. She tried to look through that imperturbable composure of his, and wondered if he knew that her heart was pounding, that her legs felt weak and her eyes were dark with unease. From the corner of her eye she noticed another figure standing near them. It was one of the Servants. It walked close behind her, watching her, assuring that she did not cause any more disturbances. Adelene held back her tears and swallowed hard. The man did not let go of her arm until she stepped into the carriage. "You shall be home shortly," he repeated. He gave her a polite nod, and closed the door securely.

24 ERRONEOUS

Etienne was sitting on the edge of one of the long steps that led to the university building, his legs crossed in front of him. He held a transparent book reader in one hand, and in the other he held a pen that he clicked repetitively against the step he sat on. When the girl walked up to him, he was too plunged in his reading to notice.

"Hey," she said.

He looked up and took his headphones off.

"You're Etienne, right?"

"Yeah," he answered. He wasn't sure he had ever seen her before.

She looked at him coldly. In the rays of the Lights, her eyes were a pale hazel color, like that of the light that seeped through the maple leaves in autumn. She had thin features and long blond hair that lined her tall, harmonious figure.

"What are you reading?" she asked placidly. She didn't tell him her name.

"Just a book for school. It's kind of boring actually." He smiled but the girl did not smile back and it made him feel stupid.

Over her shoulder she held a belted bridle bag and he watched her open it and take out a small beige book that he recognized instantly. "Is this yours?" she asked.

"Hey! Where did you find that?" he snapped, reaching out to take it from her.

The girl moved her hand away from him. "Who's Montesquieu?" she asked.

Etienne shook his head. "That book is mine. Give it back."

"I'll give it back. But who's Montesquieu?" the girl repeated calmly.

Etienne was getting more and more uneasy. His eyes darted across the campus at everything that moved. "He was French political thinker. He wrote that book sometime around seventeen forty-eight."

"What is it about?"

"Never mind what it's about," he retorted. "It doesn't matter. Please give me my book back."

She hid the book behind her back. "Come with me," she said.

"Who are you?"

"Come with me if you want your book back."

Etienne stood up without a word and followed her down the long steps and out onto the street of Anderson. The girl did not wait for him as she crossed the street and walked into the leafy park beyond. She did not follow the path. She walked up to a tree and waited for him there, with a composure that made him nervous. She looked at him as he walked towards her submissively, his schoolbag flung casually over his shoulder.

"Look," he sighed, leaning closer to her to whisper, "I don't know who you are, but if you're trying to get both of us arrested, you're on the right track."

"This is a banned book," the girl said with a sly smirk on her lips.

Etienne looked around fretfully. "Yes," he acquiesced calmly, "it is."

"Is that why you decided to burn this one?" The girl with the hazel eyes plunged her hand in her bag again and gently pulled out a blackened book, its pages frayed by fire.

The boy's eyes widened. His hands were shaking. He did not answer.

"Why would you decide to burn your own books?"

"I didn't burn anything," he affirmed.

"So who did?"

Again there was no answer.

"Is it because you were scared?"

"I didn't burn those books," he repeated, his dark eyes fixed onto hers. He wished she would go away. He wished she could leave him alone. He didn't like her way of staring at him as if she could control him with her eyes. Why did she have those books with her? Who was she anyway? "I don't know what you want from me," he said.

"I want to know why you burned the books."

"Why do you want to know *anything* about these books? Why do they interest you so much? And why do you expect me to tell you anything if I don't even know who you *are*?"

"Because I need to know."

Etienne sighed. "Forget those books. They won't bring you anywhere. They won't bring you anything but the worse of trouble. If I were you I would shut up and try to stay out of it."

"Try to stay out of it? That's what everybody 'tries' to do. Everybody's scared to stand up and change things because everyone's a coward."

"We can't change things." Etienne cast his eyes down at the bogus grass under the shadow of the tree.

"Don't pretend to think I don't know what I'm saying," the girl snapped, "I read those books of yours. On the shelf in the shed, in the Twenty-First. We all did. All five of us."

Etienne looked up at her, his gaze trapped between curiosity and distrust. "Who is 'us'?"

"The only ones in this world who admit the obvious. The only ones who don't crouch away from the fact that there's something dreadfully wrong about our world, and who won't just stand around, putting up with their miserable lives, as they wait for someone else to act. And if you ever want your book back, Rhynes," she said, her hazel eyes grasping onto his, "you'll have to decide which side your on."

"You're making a big mistake," Etienne rejoined, "I won't be part of this. Give me the book."

Suddenly she clutched his arm firmly with her hand and dragged him up the hill that rose to their left among the trees. For the first time, he noticed there was someone else with them, a tall, robust shadow following in silence. Had he been following them all along? The girl dragged him on until they reached the foot of the West Wall, looming far up into the clouds.

"Can you please tell me what the hell you're doing?" he asked, panting. He seemed angrier now. She looked at him coldly, and didn't let go of him. From the corner of his eye Etienne could see the somber face of the girl's friend, half-hidden under a large hood. It was rigid and impassive.

"Touch the Wall, Rhynes," the girl said, staring at Etienne confidently.

He looked at the boy next to him, then at the girl, confused. "What?"

"Do what she says," the other one added. He had a slow, imperturbable voice.

Etienne obeyed, and then drew his hand back. A cold shiver ran up his spine.

"What do you feel?" the girl asked, her voice more bitter than before.

"It's cold."

"It's a horrible feeling, isn't it? Frightening even, don't you think?" She spoke so quietly and so close to his face that he could feel her breaths in his ear. "I'll tell you what it is you feel, Rhynes. It's a barrier. It's imprisonment, limitation, injustice. What you feel when you touch that Wall is just how wrong our entire World is." There was sudden calmness to her voice when the last few words passed through her lips, as if her anger had given way to some other feeling, an inscrutable feeling deep in the impenetrable shadows of her mind. "And these Walls you hesitate to touch aren't the most frightening. There are worse walls here. Suffocating walls that confine our minds, shielding our eyes from terrible truths, forcing us to burry our resistance in little stone boxes deep inside us. And who hides behind all this? A cowardly little man with a voice as strong as steel."

"And what do you want me to do about it?" He said crossly.

"You have to start using your *brain* to break down the walls." With these words she kissed him curtly on the cheek and let go of his hand, and walked away nonchalantly across the field towards the houses, her companion following her silently. The boy looked quickly back at Etienne over his shoulder, his eyes shielded by the shadow of his hood and his hands shoved in his pockets, and then both of them disappeared in the foliage.

Bewildered, Etienne stepped back from the Wall, his left hand still cold from its eerie touch. "Hey!" he called after the girl, "You said you'd give me my book back!"

A bird whistled somewhere in the trees.

Silence.

25 GUNSHOT

The man moved closer to her and forced his voice down to a soft, tender pleading. "Stay with me, Dysde."

Pathetic, she thought. He disgusted her. He twirled a lock of her golden hair gently between his fingers and stared wantonly at her lips. She jerked her head away. "Is this not what you want?" He asked, calmly.

She looked deep into his eyes. "You're a coward," she said.

The man turned his back to her and stared through the high glass window. The setting sun left red stains in the clouds that moved slowly over the mountains. He took a few nonchalant steps closer to the window and stood there silently. The leopard came to sit quietly at his feet. He stroked the animal's speckled brow and lifted the glass to his lips. "You're a rash, stubborn woman, Dysde," he said, his lips curved into a faint smirk, "That is what I love about you."

"You are incapable of loving," he heard her say in her calm, fearless voice. "You are a coward and a tyrant."

"All men are. You of all women should know that."

"I of all women refuse to be the slave of a man like

you."

He clenched his fist around the diamond pendant. Slowly, he turned back around and stared at her with those cold, wolfish eyes of his. "You know that no man has ever risen to power as quickly as I have. If you accept me, all of that power will be yours as well." "But if you refuse me, nothing can stop me from use it against you."

"You don't know me."

"I know you well enough. I know why you came on this ship. You think you can leave your past behind, but who have you fooled? You've convinced them that you'd changed, but you're still the wretched woman you were. An irreparably low, shameless creature."

"You're wrong. I may have led a life that I regret, but I boarded this ship because I wanted to give my daughter a chance."

"Ah yes, the little Sara. What a lovely child. Perhaps under the care of the Nurses she will not grow up to be as troublesome and impetuous a woman as you."

"Under the care of the Nurses?"

"My voice is the Law, my dear Dysde. I can strip you of everything you hold dear with a lift of the finger. If you refuse me, your daughter will learn to despise you, as will all of the habitants of this ship, while you rot miserably in prison, as was your fate on Earth." He walked up to her and whispered in her ear, "No one disobeys me."

In the blink of an eye she drew a small knife from the belt at her waist and held it to his neck.

The man smiled. "What have we here? Ah, Dysde, always full of surprises."

"I will never go back to prison. Never!"

The man made a quick gesture with his hand, and the leopard pounced at her with a growl and knocked the knife from her hand. She fell to the ground, four deep cuts running up her left arm.

"As you wish," the man said calmly. He pulled a small revolver from his belt, calmly, silently, and pointed it at her.

Eyes wide with fear, she stood up and rushed to the doors. They were locked. She pressed her body against them, pounded against them with her fists. She turned back around, horrified. "You monster!" she cried out.

"I'm sorry, Dysde," he said. And he pulled the trigger. The grisly sound of the gunshot, concealed behind the impenetrable palace walls, hushed not a single bird in the trees, nor troubled the tranquil water in the stone basins of the gardens. Silently, the Servants carried the body away.

26 FALSE

Adelene sat on the green wooden chair in her room and leaned onto the windowsill, looking out at the sleeping village with pensive eyes.

Why isn't he back?

Her eyes gleamed in the glowering light of the candle at her side. She felt its gentle fragrance sticking to her cheeks. Olio wasn't back. Maybe he had been caught after all. She tried to force the dark thoughts out again, but every time she did they came back.

Where are you, Olio?

The flame danced and sighed as it bathed in the tranquil pool of melted wax. She could see its distorted refection in the glass window, sinking away, ghostlike, into the night. She pressed her forehead against the window and looked at the stars. She could see Emmeline's face in her mind, cold, distant, the green eyes fixed onto hers. She saw the guard pushing the group of young girls back into the hallway. She saw the man with the grey suit forcing her into the carriage that drove her back to the doorstep of her house like a prisoner, without explanation. And Emmeline had disappeared again.

Her door was closed and it was soundless in Adelene's room. Motionless. Lành was in bed, probably reading one of his adventure books. Or perhaps he was asleep by now. Then a little voice called her name indistinctly, and there was a hesitant knock at the door. It was Lành. Adelene stood up with a lazy exhale and opened the door.

"Adelene?" her brother murmured in a drowsy voice.

"What's wrong, Lành? You should be in bed."

"Can you come say goodnight to me?"

Adelene leaned onto the doorway. "Can't I say goodnight to you *here*?"

The boy looked at her with saddened eyes that gleamed in the dim light of the hallway. "But—but Mommy usually comes to my room to say goodnight." His thin white socks blended with the carpet under his feet. The walls had a soft smell of incense.

"I know, I know," Adelene said, yawning. Her yawn turned into a yielding sigh as she took Lành's hand into hers. The two of them walked quietly to the little boy's room, and Adelene sat on the edge of the bed. Lành smiled as she tucked Fox under the covers next to him. Fox was a fluffy red panda with eyes made out of black marbles. It had a small bell that tinkled on a navy blue collar sewn into its neck.

"I really miss her," Lành said.

Adelene stroked his hand. "I miss her too, Lành, but she will be back soon."

"When?"

"Myrna said a couple of days, but not long. Mom is really busy, you know."

Lành turned onto his side, wrinkling the covers. "While you were in your room, I thought I heard her voice downstairs," he mumbled.

"You did?"

"Yeah." He nodded.

"Well, she isn't back yet, but she will soon. You have to go to sleep, now, O.K?"

"What was that?" he gasped suddenly.

Adelene looked over her shoulder at the open door, then back at Lành. "What was what?"

"I heard a voice again, Adelene."

"Whose voice?"

"Mommy's voice. Downstairs." He sat up and leaned over to look out the door.

"Wait, no! Lành, Myrna's still up!"

"But I want to go see!" He whispered.

"Lành, she won't like it if she sees that you're still awake. You have to go back to bed. Mommy's not back."

"Will she be back soon?"

Adelene sighed. "Yes," she said, "Soon. Now, lie down. You're very tired, that's all. When we're tired, we don't think clearly. You have to close your eyes and let your thoughts go away, like train wagons passing by. Don't hold on to them. Go to sleep."

Lành nodded and closed his eyes. "Goodnight, Adelene," he mumbled under the soft quilt.

"Goodnight, Lành." She kissed him on the forehead and slowly walked out of the room and closed the door halfway behind her.

"Wait—Can you close it all the way?"

"Sure," she whispered with a soft smile. And she closed the door quietly, all the way. She waited there until she was sure her brother had fallen asleep and wouldn't call her anymore, and then she tiptoed back to her room. She paused in the doorway and listened intensely for any sounds from downstairs. A deep silence answered her. She shivered and closed the door.

It was cold that night. She coughed in the sleeve of her sweater and sat on her bed, and looked at the empty chair by the window. She didn't want to sleep. She wanted to know what had happened to Olio. Was he hiding somewhere, waiting for Them to give up Their search? Was he being permanently deactivated by the Onweald, right here as she was thinking it, never to see her again?

For five years she had managed, somehow, to keep him hidden. Now he was gone, and she was lost among haunting thoughts, guilt ridden and alone. She never should have let him lead her like that. She should have known better. She should have ordered him to take her home the minute she had seen when he was taking her. Olio cared about her. When she was sad, it made him sad. When she smiled, his eyes gleamed with happiness. She loved the little robot because he had a soul. When she looked into his eyes she felt a connection—a deep, human connection—like the one you feel when you hold someone's hand. Olio didn't belong in the Laboratories.

Lying down on her bed, Adelene tried to wash the thoughts away. Her mind began its gradual fall into the current of disarrayed images that begins all dreams, and she dozed of into a half-conscious somnolence, enveloped in the darkness under her eyelids. She did not want to dream. Dreams were cursed. It was bad to have dreams. But slowly, gently, she let herself fall into their grasp.

Emmeline's face materialized in her mind. She could see the soft green eyes and wavy blond hair whirled into a loose bun, the pendant of pure diamond around her neck, the flowing white dress dotted with golden beads, a shawl of translucent silk, flowing like waves—waves—like the glimmering Ocean.

The Ocean.

It danced across her vision, and the green-eyed girls danced in the waves and began to sing.

It's beautiful, Daddy… It's so beautiful. She was a young girl again. She watched the waves.

Her father's voice echoed in her mind. *It is a film about the ocean. I told you about the ocean.* She could see him. She could see him clearly in the dream. Was it a dream? In her father's eyes, there were tears, glistening like the Ocean where Emmeline danced. *I want you to have the Memories.* It was a white screen in a bundle of woven fabric. *I want you to know the world you are from.* She felt his loving kiss against her cheek. Darkness. A figure standing in the doorway. A needle in her arm. Myrna.

She gasped and opened her eyes. It was just a dream. She lifted herself to a seated position, and covered her face with trembling hands. Her forehead was moist with sweat and the room felt stuffy. *Only a dream*, she thought. The image of her father and the small white screen in its sheath of woven fabric refused to ebb from her mind, trapped there like a bad thought. The Ocean. The needle. *It shoos out all the bad thoughts in your mind*, she heard Myrna say, *and replaces them with good thoughts.* A poignant fear crawled up her spine. The voices, the waves, the robotic eyes, the syringe in Myrna's hand—it all felt so real. It trapped her—locked her in—as would a dreadful, forgotten memory suddenly remembered.

She could hear a voice in the darkness.

It was not Lành's voice. It was a clear, smooth voice—her mother's voice—and it came from downstairs.

Adelene slipped out of her room without a sound, her sweater zipped up to her neck and her hands tucked in her sleeves. She peered into Lành's room—maybe the voice came from the hologram transmitter that he kept by his desk—but the boy lay fast asleep and the transmitter was turned off. She closed the door and tiptoed down the stairs. The steps groaned under her feet a little, but not loud enough to reach Myrna's audio discerners.

The voice came again, but this time it was Myrna's voice. "Activate sound reproduction," it said, "Copy voice. Jade Harlow intonation. Hologram. Replay."

Adelene held her breath and crouched behind the staircase. The door to Myrna's closet was wide open behind the dining room. It was empty. There was a faint light coming from the small hallway behind the staircase, the one that led from the open kitchen to her mother's room. Adelene crept across the living room. The light from the hallway was so clear that she could see her reflection in the wall of glass that faced the garden across the living room. She moved along the wall, closer and closer to the light and the voices.

"Goodnight, Lành," her mother's voice sounded faintly from the lit hallway, "I will be back soon… Go to sleep now… I love you, sweetheart."

Adelene peered around the corner and blinked in the light. The door to her mother's room was half-open. She caught a glimpse of Myrna's silhouette behind it and walked soundlessly up to the door. She looked through the opening. Myrna stood in front of the holographic image of Adelene's mother, her laser eyes emitting a sharp blue light, staring strait into the figure in the hologram.

"Program voice," Myrna said, *"Go to sleep, Lành."*

"Go to sleep, Lành," the hologram of her mother echoed. The image flickered.

"Trigger response," Myrna said to it, "Advanced voice replication. Jade Harlow." The transmitter beeped.

Adelene felt her heart sink as if she had been hurled down a dark precipice. "Myrna!" she shrieked, barging into the room.

The android's eyes darted towards the open door and stared at Adelene with a look of unreserved shock. It was an inhuman look. Almost wolfish.

"What are you doing?" Adelene gasped, "Are you encoding the hologram?"

Myrna did not answer.

"You've programmed it all along? All those nights, it

127

wasn't Mom saying goodnight to Lành from Filmur, it was *you*?"

Myrna started coldly at the girl. "It is late, Miss Adelene. You must go to bed."

"Where is she?" Adelene snapped defiantly. "She isn't on a professional trip. You lied, didn't you? You lied to us!"

"Disobedient girl." Slowly, the android took a step closer to her.

Adelene took a step back. Suddenly, the image in her dream came back to her—the slender figure in the doorway. The gleaming, threatening eyes. "Where are they, Myrna? My mother *and* my father."

Upon hearing that last word, the android's face twisted into a grotesque, startled expression. "Your father is dead."

"He isn't! I know he isn't!" Adelene cried out. "You're the one who took him from us, aren't you? I saw it in a dream. The needle. You made me forget."

The android's eyes burned like flames. "Have you lost your mind, Miss Adelene? How *dare* you question me!"

"You have no right to hide this from us! I command you to tell me where my parents are!"

Myrna leaped at her. She wrapped an arm around her neck and pressed the other hand against the girl's mouth to muffle her screams. Adelene's eyes were wide with terror. She tried to pull Mryna's arm away from her, she kicked and shook her head, and tried to scream again. She felt trapped in the arms of a shadowy stone monster, an outlandish, pallid creature with limbs of steel. Myrna was strong. Very strong. And her fingers were hard and cold like long, thick needles.

Myrna whispered in her ear, "*You deny my authority, you deny His.*"

Suddenly there came a crashing sound from the window on the far side of the room, and Olio came stumbling through the broken glass and into the room. Adelene felt

Myrna's arms lose their grip around her neck and mouth, and then let her go altogether in surprise. The robot jumped onto Myrna, and in a flash he struck her down with his fist.

"Olio!" Adelene shouted. A smile of relief rose to her lips. "Olio, you're back!"

The robot looked down at Myrna's inert body. "Hurry, Adelene! I have to get you out of here. We don't have much time."

"It's alright. I think you knocked her down pretty hard."

"I'm not talking about Myrna. I mean the Police Droids, Adelene. They're coming. I'm being tracked. They will be here any minute now."

"What?" she yelped, "They're tracking you?"

"I was captured, Adelene. They captured me and placed a tracking mechanism on my back. They want to know who is hiding me from Them!"

"Turn around."

Olio turned around. It was a little black device no bigger than a fingernail, protruding from the android's left shoulder bone. "I tried to tear it off. It won't come off."

"Hold on." Adelene ran to the kitchen and groped around in the darkness for the utensil drawer. Behind the counter she heard the tetchy grumbling of a Cleaner. It must have been activated by the sudden noises and had trouble deactivating itself again. She grabbed a large kitchen knife and ran back down the hall and into the room.

"Turn around, Olio."

"What are you doing?"

"Don't move," she said.

"What are you doing?"

"I said, don't move!" Adelene raised the knife up above her head and flung it down onto Olio's back, closing her eyes as the blade came crashing down onto the little black device. There was an electrical flicker, a tiny blue light. She had sliced it in half. "There," she said with a proud grin, "I think it's broken."

Sirens howled somewhere nearby. It was a quiet howl, a low droning, distant and yet so close. It rose stealthily into the night air, like a secret sound that only they could here. The village was asleep.

"I can sense their approach, Adelene. They're coming. Hurry!" Olio grabbed her by the arm, dragged her to the front door and forced it open. The air was cool and dry. It had an earthy, leafy smell.

"Adelene?" A little voice came from inside the house. It was Lành.

Adelene stopped and wrung her arm out of Olio's grip. "Olio, Lành is still inside! I can't leave him!"

"He'll be alright," Olio answered, taking her arm again, "We have to go."

"Go where, Olio?"

"Hide."

"Where?"

"Somewhere. Anywhere. Hurry! Lành will be fine."

"No, They'll take him! We have to go back and get him!"

"They're not after him, Adelene."

"They'll take anyone they can find in this house. *Please*, Olio! Let me go back." She tried to pull herself away, but his grip was firm this time. "They took Mom and Dad!" There were tears in her eyes. They glistened in the darkness, blurs of reflected light from some obscure source nearby. Maybe it was just the night-Lights reflected in her tears. "I won't let them take Lành!"

"I'll go then," Olio said. He hesitated, looked around, and finally let go of her hand. "Thank you," she sniveled, watching as he turned back towards the house without a word, his eyes gleaming in the darkness.

"Go," he whispered, looking at her one last time. "Hide. Anywhere. I'll come find you."

Adelene ran silently across the street and hid in the obscurity of the trees that lined a neighboring house. It felt strangely silent among the trees, as if they too had been looking for her, waiting for the right moment to wrap their long, twisted branches around her and trap her there forever. She shivered. Peering out, she watched on as a multitude of black shadows crowded around the house. They looked like dark, flying orbs with eyes and arms barging in through the doors and windows, droning, droning, and the silent sirens sounding, like a noise inside her head, like muffled echoes in a nightmare. The village was fast asleep.

There was a cry from inside. It was Lành. *Please don't take him away,* Adelene whispered, forcing her eyes shut. *Please don't take my little brother.*

She recognized his little voice—that innocent little voice. Frightened.

Please. Please. Please. Olio, save him!

Suddenly, something jumped out of the shadows and stood in the middle of the road. As it approached the glow of the streetlamp the slender silhouette materialized slowly. It was Myrna. "I know you are here, Miss Adelene," she said, scrutinizing every shrub, every blade of grass with sharp precision. Her voice was spasmodic and there was a large dent in her metallic scalp, where Olio had struck. Her left eye was inoperative.

Adelene crouched behind the trees.

"You cannot escape," Myrna's voice came again. "I will find you." It was closer now—as close as the darkness.

She had to run. She had to run now. The wind howled in the trees. The sirens sounded again, a distant hum. Lành's voice had vanished. Adelene darted out from behind the trees. She sped across the lawn, through a gravel path, then across lawn again. Only one idea crossed her mind: Reach the transport station. Hide.

The entrance to the transport station was at the end of the street. She could hear Myrna's footsteps—rapid thuds against the wet grass, against the gravel behind her. The Lights of the night watched on like gleaming eyes above the village. Adelene ran across the road and reeled down the stairs of the entranceway, met with the sounds of the trains on the rails and the cars in the tunnels, and the gush of air that slithered from the tunnels and across the platforms. Middleton was a discreet little town. The platforms were empty.

Adelene ran without thinking. It was as if her feet had decided to keep on running and would never stop, pulling her down to the lower levels of the station. The flowing voices in the moving images that illuminated the walls echoed faintly. Voices sounded everywhere, and yet the station was empty. The low, peaceful feminine voice that reverberated in the darkish platform seemed to address itself to ghosts: *The doors are now closing. Please stand clear of the doors.*

"Wait!" Adelene screamed, "No! Let me in! Help!"

From the corner of her eye Adelene saw something crawl recklessly down the stairs, a shadowy and nimble thing that blended with the whitish, platinum ground. It was Myrna. The android's good eye darted frantically across the platform and fixed onto the girl. Adelene felt her heart jump to her throat. She wanted to scream. She wanted to cry out. But who would hear? Who would help?

Four minutes and twenty-two seconds until next local train to Westerly, Eighteenth Division. The train began to advance, sluggish and indifferent. She never knew what pushed her to do what she did next. Perhaps it was fear, the feeling of being utterly disarmed and defeated, sudden sensation that the world was collapsing inward, that there was no other choice. Her hand wrapped firmly around the bar between the closed doors of the train wagon. She found a foothold and did not move. The spectral train accelerated. Adelene screamed and held on tightly as the rails underneath screeched with the weight of the moving train. Myrna leaped forward and tried to grab the girl's leg, but she was too late. *Don't let go,"* she murmured to herself, *"don't let go.* She squeezed her eyes shut and turned her face away. She did not want to see the dark mouth of the tunnel approaching, looming over her, and then finally engulfing her. She felt her fingers clasp the metal bar. When she opened her eyes again she could feel the darkness, the greyish coldness of that vast chasm of noise and commotion that had swallowed her. The train moved fast—very fast—and with every sudden jolt of the wheels she felt herself clutching harder. The train began to smoothen its course, advancing in a strait trajectory between the wide walls of the tunnel. The pace was calmer now, the noise more even. Even the screeching of the rails had ceased. Adelene looked over her shoulder. The mouth of the tunnel was far behind her now, a pale stain of light in a world of darkness and mechanical noise. Myrna was nowhere to be seen. Adelene felt the rhythmic thudding of the train against the tracks.

There was an abrupt jolt, the train shrieked and the tunnel widened. Dull ceiling lights flashed past in repetitious sequence—light and dark, light and dark—a quick alternation of clarity and gloom, too quick to immerse her entirely in one or the other. There was only one place left in the world where she could find shelter: the Twenty-First Division. She had to jump off at Anderson University and make for the forested hills beyond the northern outlet, hide in the abandoned shed and stay there through the night. That was the only way.

Station platforms stretched on either side of the multiple tracks. Adelene caught a glimpse of an indication on the arched walls: *Lyvemore, Division Twenty-Four.* The train did not slow down. And then the tunnel shrunk again and all was darkness and furious sound. Would the train stop at Anderson? Her feet were slipping but she dared not move them for fear of falling. She felt the blisters forming in the palms of her hands. How much longer could she hold?

Maybe it was all just a nightmare. Maybe soon she would wake up and find herself back in her warm bed, and all of this would be over. But such a thought was useless. All of her senses were awake and alert. The numbness in her feet from the aggressive shuddering of the train, the stiffness in her pallid fingers grasping the metal bar between its doors, the deafening noise of the rails in her ears, the blurry darkness, the earthy smell of the tunnel, the sickly taste of fear. And there was something else too. A feeling that only fear creates so vividly: the feeling that she was not alone. She felt a presence other than her own—a strange, frightening presence—somewhere, somehow.

She turned her head towards the back of the train, where the tracks receded into the darkness like a shadowy snake, and her heart jumped. From one of the dark slits between the many train cars that formed the corpus of the train, a globular eye of piercing brightness stared back at her. It was Myrna's eye.

Myrna was on the train.

27 HAZE

The android's spidery silhouette slinked silently closer and closer, crawling nimbly along the side of the train cars, from one car to the next. Adelene was too frightened to scream. She could not run. She could not yell for help. She stood petrified against the moving train, her face pale and her eyes wide with fear. There was nothing to do but to hold on tightly, and to wait for the light of the Anderson University station to appear at the end of the tunnel—a speck of light, a speck of hope. On either side of the train the walls of the tunnel sunk away, as if they were being sucked into a chasm. It seemed endless, that hollow murk through which the noises of the rails were trapped, through which the train sped furiously, on and on forever, like a giant segmented worm buried in the complex sublevels of the ship. Adelene watched Myrna creeping closer, her metallic body camouflaged against the lifeless machine. Myrna clung onto the walls of the speeding train feverishly, her gaze fixed onto Adelene. Could she hurt her?

The stealthy figure was very close now—so close that Adelene could see the hazy fleck of shattered metal that had once been the android's eye. Would she hurt her?

Could Myrna kill her? Adelene tried to move her feet a little further along the rim on which they lay, but it was useless.

Then a boom of light swept across her face, and with it a gush of wind, and the mouth of the tunnel disappeared behind them as the train slowed into the station and screeched to a stop. On either side of the platform the arched walls read, *Anderson University, Division Twenty-Two.* Adelene jumped off and stumbled across the platform through the ghostly crowd, through the light and noise, pushing her way through the nebulous mass of heads and jackets, a sea of prudent figures gathered busily along the tracks. Myrna darted furiously after her, crawling up the walls and across the ceiling above, as stealthily as a phantom, as soundless as a shadow.

Below the dull hum of voices and the whistling of the trains lay a deep and unobtrusive silence. It breathed through the walls and came to lie among the shadows. It was there in the steam that hissed through broken valves, whose dark forms slithered along the walls and between the tracks.

Could anyone else hear the silence?

Adelene staggered up the metal staircase and stumbled out, once again, into the night air. There was no time to look back. There was no time to think. Her eyes darted in all directions, looking for a familiar sight. Streetlights lined the campus of the university, tinting the many silhouettes in a yellow glow against the night. The light poured over the gravel path beneath their feet and the wind made the leaves sing in the dark trees above. A hazy, aromatic mist seeped onto the street from a noisy restaurant. A dog growled and a woman clasped her hat to her head as Adelene darted past them. Cheerful music spurred from a small café and with it laughter and voices, and then faded away behind her.

She ran towards the southern outlet, beyond which

stood the forested hills of the Twenty-First Division. She would find shelter in the darkness there, beyond the lights of Anderson. She ran so fast that she could barely feel her feet touching the ground.

The great passage between the divisions seemed to cast a dark and ominous shadow on the tranquil streets. Adelene ran on. A bitter dryness in her lungs scorched every breath she took. The last townhouse sunk away behind her and trees seemed to crowd around her. A flash of metal caught her eye; Myrna's silhouette slithered through the darkness, crawled between the branches and hid among the leaves. The android had not lost sight of its target. It was there, so close to her, and yet it did not seize her. It was following her—only following. Soon, Adelene knew, fatigue would overcome her and she would fall helplessly to the ground.

The Wall towered above, a limitless barrier stretching between the two Divisions. Adelene soared through the great outlet along the small road that sliced through it and stumbled among the calm hills of Twenty-First Division. Her breaths burned her lungs and her legs felt heavier and heavier the more she ran. The trees that grew in clusters around the hidden shelter materialized like a shadowy haze under the soft white glow of the night-Lights. At the top of that hill was the secret place—the place that had to be kept hidden from Them at all costs—and she was leading Myrna strait to it. The thought overwhelmed her. There was nowhere to run to anymore.

Exhausted, Adelene dropped down on her stomach among the high grasses and buried her face in her arms. Maybe the darkness would conceal her. There was nothing left to trust but the darkness. The earth smelled of stagnant humidity. A shadow crept up behind her.

A strong hand grabbed her leg. She screamed and tried to squirm free but the android turned her onto her back and pinned her to the ground. Cold fingers wrapped around the soft warm flesh of the girl's neck, and just as they began squeezing tighter, Adelene knew. Myrna was going to kill her.

Her body struggled and she tried to scream again, but she could neither breathe nor make a sound. She was helpless, exhausted, and at the mercy of the one who had raised her and protected her for as long as she could remember. She starred blankly into the blinding light of Myrna's eye. *Please,* she tried to say. Her head was pounding from fear and lack of air. *Please...* but her lips only quivered slightly. In response the android's hands squeezed tighter around her throat. The world seamed to spin around her. The darkness crawled into her eyes.

Suddenly a loud zapping sound tore through the silence and something collapsed by her side. Adelene gasped for breath and lifted her head off the ground. Inches from her face lay Myrna's distorted visage, the blue light from its one remaining eye twitching like a broken electric circuit.

28 NIGHT

Adelene could not repress another scream of horror. She touched her hands to her reddened throat and coughed, then gasped again. The android's hand reached out towards the girl's face in a last effort to grasp hold of its prey, then the arm collapsed to the ground and the light from the eye faded out entirely. Adelene stared at the inert figure with petrified eyes, still struggling to catch her breath.

"Are you alright?" said a low voice coming from somewhere in the obscurity, "Calm down. It's dead. It can't hurt you anymore." She suddenly became conscious of a tall figure moving towards her in the darkness. The figure bent down next to her and tried to help her up.

"Let go of me!" She blurted out, her voice trembling and her eyes wide with fear.

"I'm not going to hurt you," the voice said. It was a young man's voice. She couldn't tell how old he was. She looked up at him. Her eyes were used to the darkness now, and in the soft glow of the night-Lights she recognized him. It was Etienne Rhynes.

"I know you," he said, smiling, "You're Adelene Harlow. You go to Middleton School, don't you? I used to go there. I'm Etienne by the way. Etienne Rhynes."

He held a gun in his hand, a small black gun that he pointed carefully downwards. Adelene had never seen a gun before, let alone in a human hand. She looked up at him, then back at Myrna's inert body. "You killed her," she said in a broken voice, almost a whisper. "You killed her."

"I guess you could say that. Although those things aren't ever really alive to begin with."

Her eyes remained fixed on the deformed features of the Familiar. "But how—You can't—How—"

"Here, take my hand," he said kindly, holding out the palm of his hand. "I'll help you up." She took it hesitantly, staring at the gun, and got up. Then she watched him lift the stolid mass of metal in his arms, grimacing under its weight, and carry it to the edge of the pond. An owl hooted somewhere in the trees. He pushed the android into the murky black water and watched it sink to the bottom. Getting down on his knees, he scooped handfuls of muddy earth from the bank and threw them into the water where the android's limbs still shone under the light of the stars. The night-Lights gleamed palely, too, between the Walls and the great Window, casting long shadows across the hills.

Adelene's throat burned and her legs were numb. She coughed in the sleeve of her shirt as Etienne led her up the hill and into the wooden shed. He held one arm reassuringly around her shoulders, and the warmth of his touch comforted her. She noticed a strange object around his wrist—a small, circular timepiece at the center of a leather band. It looked much like a watch, but a peculiar one, outlandish, antique, *Earthly*. He sat her down onto the wooden stool and handed her a water bottle. She drank thirstily, watching the reddened ashes in the fire.

"I'm sorry it's so cold here," Etienne said, "I can't make the fire too noticeable."

"It's better than outside," Adelene said with a small laugh. "Besides, a little cold feels good after running for so long."

"I bet. Why were you running from her? Did you steal or something?"

The tears in her eyes glistened in the low firelight. "They have my parents. And my brother."

"Detained?" He asked. Adelene couldn't find a word to describe his reaction. Shocked? Angry? Concerned? She nodded in reply, as more tears welled in her eyes and fell in warm droplets along her cheeks. She wiped them off with the back of her hand. Etienne knelt down next to her. "It'll be alright," he said. She knew he did not know what else to say. "You need some rest. Don't worry, you're safe here."

"But Lành isn't safe!" she cried out, "I was supposed to watch over him! I saw the Police take him away but I had no choice but to run! I had no choice but to—" Grief chocked her voice and she let her face fall into the palms of her hands.

"Adelene, listen to me. Tomorrow morning, we'll find a solution, but for now you need to let it go. You need to rest. There's nothing else you can do."

Something whimpered in a corner of the room. A large black muzzle peered out of the shadows and sniffed its way to her feet. A large dog with a sleek golden fleece stared up at her with friendly eyes.

Etienne scowled. "Henry!" The dog's ears jerked back at the sound of the word. "Sorry, it's my dog. He loves people."

Henry rose up onto his hind legs and placed both paws on Adelene's lap. Adelene smiled meekly and stroked his soft golden fur. For a moment, the nightmarish darkness disappeared from her thoughts, but then the smile bled into a sob. A tear rolled smoothly from her eyes. "I just wish there was a way out of this."

"We'll find a way. I'll help you. Don't worry. Please. Just try to let yourself rest."

She nodded. She felt ashamed to be crying and wiped her eyes.

"So you're with the blond girl." He was smiling a little, but his voice held a slight trace of touchiness.

"Sara?"

"Is that her name? Sara? Fits her pretty well."

"You know her?"

He shook his head. "She seemed to know *me*. She came up to me in Anderson a couple of days ago and asked me about the books."

"The banned books?"

He nodded and took some time to answer. "Yeah. That's how I knew I wasn't the only one who had found this place." He paused, waiting for her to say something, but she didn't. He was glad she didn't. "How long have you been coming here?"

"Just a few days, actually. Sorry. We didn't think it belonged to anyone."

"Nah," he said, "No reason to be sorry. I haven't been here in months." His voice trailed off and he seemed to lose himself in his thoughts.

"What made you come back?" she asked in a shy voice.

Etienne shrugged nonchalantly. For a while his eyes avoided hers. He sat down with his hands locked together in front of his knees and looked down at the floor. "As a kid, have you ever snuck up to the attic in your house out of curiosity, where you knew nobody could see or hear you—not the Authorities, not your parents, not anyone but whoever you brought there with you—and decided that it would be your secret place?"

"The place where you could hide all your little treasures and say all your dreams out loud?" Adelene forced her face into a smile, but she could feel the tears clogged up in her throat. The thought of the attic brought back the thought of her father.

Etienne laughed. "Yeah, *that* place. Where there's no one to spy on you. No one to tell you what to think. But then—" He paused, and stared up at the ceiling. "Then there's this fear of the dark that never really leaves you. You never stay too long in the attic, because sooner or later the darkness starts to crowd around you and bring up all the bad memories and all the bad dreams in your head. And then one day your foot gets caught on a shard in the wooden planks that line the floor and you're hurt bad, but you're afraid to tell anyone how you got hurt, because then They'd know your secret and you'd get punished for going into the attic. So you painfully endure it, you hide the wound until it slowly heals by itself, and you promise yourself you'll never again go back to the attic. Never again to the harmful wooden shards and the darkness that revives bad dreams. You promise yourself you'll never disobey again.

"This shed is like that for me. It recalls things I want to forget. Things I wish had never happened. Things that happened by my fault." He scratched Henry behind the ear and the animal closed his eyes blithely. "That's why I told myself I'd never come back. But places like this are hard to forget. You can try, but sooner or later you'll start to miss the freedom it gave you. You'll miss what it really meant to you. You'll want to remember the reason why you decided to go there in the first place." He looked up at her. "All I needed was someone to remind me."

Adelene smiled. "Well," she said quietly, "I'm glad you decided to come back. I don't know what would've happened to me if you hadn't been there with your—your gun."

Etienne grinned slightly. He flipped the mysterious pistol around his finger and said nothing. Adelene wondered how he could possibly have gotten his hands on such a thing.

Suddenly, Henry's ears twitched again. The dog turned his head towards the door and gave a sharp growl.

"What's the matter, boy?" Etienne said, "You hear something?"

It was pitch-black through the broken window. Adelene felt a chill run through her. "What is it?"

"I don't know." Etienne walked hesitantly to the door, one hand on his pistol.

"What are you doing? Wait! Etienne!"

He slowly pushed the door open. Henry paced frantically back and forth at his feet, growling at the darkness. A dark figure stirred the murky darkness at the bottom of the hill. Henry barked. Etienne clutched the pistol.

"Adelene!" a voice cried out from the darkness. "Are you there?"

"Olio?" Adelene sprang to her feet but Etienne held her back with a strong hand.

"Stay back! That voice isn't human!"

"No! Don't shoot! He's with us!"

"*With* us?"

"I said don't shoot! Look!"

The robot's glossy features materialized in the faint glow of firelight from the shed. In its arms the robot carried a small figure, a frail little boy that grasped onto it without a sound. Etienne looked back at Adelene with confounded eyes and lowered his gun.

"Lành! Olio!" Adelene stumbled forward to meet them, her face ruffled in a mix of surprise and helpless concern. She hugged Olio and kissed her brother's cheek. The boy's eyes were closed. "How did you get away? Is he alright? Etienne shot Myrna with his gun."

"Shot her?"

"Yes. She tried to kill me. We dumped her into the lake. They won't find her there. Please tell me Lành is alright!"

"Yes, he'll be alright. He's a little stunned, but his

breathing is normal."

"How did you know where to find me?"

"I—I don't know. I just *knew*. I told you I'd come find you. I don't break promises."

He always knew. It was as if he watched over her no matter where she was—no matter how far from home, no matter how far from his sight. He was her secret guardian, a spark of humanity beneath a mechanized body. For a fraction of a second the idea lined her brow: What if Olio *was* different? What if he was not meant to Obey like the rest? What if he was there to protect them—a secret guardian that their father had re-programmed—meant to follow no one but she and Lành? It was a flicker, the ghost of a thought, forgotten even as it crossed Adelene's mind. And she hugged Olio, and smiled. "You went back for him."

Etienne stood in the doorway. He silently stepped aside to let them in. They laid Lành on a blanket by the low fire and placed a small pillow under his head.

Adelene sat down beside her brother and stroked his hair.

"Who is this?" Etienne asked.

There was a pause. Adelene hesitated. "Olio is our… house companion."

"House companion?" he shook his head in disbelief and moved closer to inspect the android. He carefully turned its head to one side, then to the other. "*House companion?* No, no, no, this isn't any kind of Service Robot; it's a government-owned versatile robot. I recognize the design. The shape of the eyes. How did you—?"

"It's a long story," she cut him off. "But he's all we have left now. He's the only one who can protect us."

Olio took her hand. "No," he said solemnly. "No, I can't."

"What do you mean?"

"I can't protect you anymore. There's only one way out of this, Adelene."

She shook her head. "What—What do you mean?"

"You have to leave."

"Leave?" Panic swelled in her heart, bringing the buried tears back to her eyes. She knew what he was about to say, in all its absurdity.

"Leave the ship, you and your brother—Listen to me!—It's the only way."

"Olio, no!"

"You have to go, Adelene." She shook her head. He took her hand in his own. "Trust me. There's no other way."

She shook her head defiantly again. "No!"

"Adelene, you know what will happen if you stay."

She stared into his eyes and held on to his gaze as if there was nothing else to hold on to. A tear rolled down her cheek and stained the wooden flooring. She knew what would happen. She had seen it, felt it in Myrna's fingers as they had clasped around her neck in the darkness. They would kill her. They would find her, and then They would kill her. The thought made her blood run cold.

It was all coming together in her head now: Her parents' disappearance, the captive girls at the Onweald's palace, Myrna's terrifying authority. And then Olio's unexplainable human side, the box with the Memories, the banned books, her dreams… She remembered Sara speaking to her in the classroom of Middleton School. *I'm not the one frightening you, Adelene.* Adelene had not made sense of those words until now. Her perfect little world was, in reality, a frightening prison of unprincipled conformity, of sameness, of Walls and Ceilings that confined the mind. And maybe her father had programed Olio not only to protect her and Lành, but to help them find the cracks in the Walls. To guide them out. Maybe this was what he had wanted all along.

Etienne stepped closer. "I'm sorry—You want her to leave the *ship*?"

"We know a way," Olio replied.

"What are you talking about? That's impossible."

"It's a passageway. Escape vessels locked in under surveillance. Meant to take you back to Earth in case of an emergency." In the firelight his beady eyes seemed to glisten just the way the tears made Adelene's eyes glisten.

"That doesn't make sense. It would take years! This ship's been gone for almost two decades! Earth is light-years away from us now."

"The escape vessels are programmed to go much faster than this ship. I modified one to go to superluminal speeds. It's an Alcubierre ship. We could make it back in a month. Maybe less."

There was a pause. Etienne stared blankly at the ground. Then he turned to Adelene. "Is this true?"

"Yes. It's true."

"Where is this passageway?"

"Flemington," she muttered, "In the Walls of Flemington."

"Inside the Walls?"

"Yes, the West Wall. It's connected to the Universal Library. The passage branches off of the Observatorium, into the restricted areas. It's a maze of dark channels and doors—extremely secretive—heavily guarded and probably even more so since—since—"

"Since what?"

"Since Olio brought me there. I saw the compartment with the vessels."

Etienne let out a puffy laugh and touched his hand to his forehead. "This is crazy."

"But it's the truth," Olio said calmly. "And if they don't leave they'll get caught. Thirty divisions—thirty kilometers—and 100,000 Authorities. Not including the

Service Robots crawling around, serving as trillions of little cameras. It's a small world. Trust me, Adelene, the Authorities will have no trouble tracking you down."

"But don't you see its impossible to go back, Olio?" she cried out. "Don't you see there's no way we could ever get through again? They've probably tripled security down there after what's happened! The Authorities aren't stupid!"

"Unless we find another way," Etienne said, staring down at the floor pensively.

"What?"

"We find another way to get you through. We find a way to shut down the Security System altogether."

Adelene coughed out a cynical, nervous laugh. "Shut down the Security System?"

"Yes. Including the microbots. The Authorities might notice the disturbance quickly, but all we need is a couple of hours."

"And how do you suppose we do *that?*"

"We can use Olio."

"No," Olio said, "I can't help you with this. I don't have access to such confidential information."

Adelene looked puzzled. "What do you mean you don't have access?"

"He doesn't know what he's saying, Adelene." Etienne said dismissively. "That reply's probably part of a security programing. Your robot's got a copy of the ship's *hard drive* right behind his eyes. He *has* to know."

"No. You don't understand. I think I've been—altered."

"Altered?" The two reacted in unison.

"When they caught me… They—They did *something*. I can't access the most confidential codes anymore. As if a part of my mind's been destroyed."

Etienne smiled in the corner of his mouth and mumbled, *Part of my mind. You don't have a mind. Just a robot.*

Adelene sighed. "Try to remember, Olio. Please! Just try.

The Central Security System—There must be a control center in some form or other—Try to remember the code to the control center."

"I—I can't," his soft, slightly metallic voice whimpered helplessly. For the first time, Olio stood in front of her as a machine, a simple automaton with programmed responses and a man-made memory easily erased. Altered. She watched him as he sat down and closed his eyes and buried his face in the palms of his stiff hands. "I can't."

The midnight bell rang in the distance, twelve low hums moving monotonously through the murky darkness. They raised their heads and strained their ears to hear it clearer, or to make sure the twelve echoing strokes weren't simply delusions of their growing fatigue. Etienne sat on the floor next to Adelene. Neither of them said a word. Time was slipping away with the night.

Then Olio made a strange sound and broke into what seemed like a series of short spasms as he sputtered, "*54349.*" He had moved to the corner of the room, by the shelf, where the shadows sliced uneven patterns along his polished composite figure.

Adelene moved towards him. "Olio?"

Etienne grabbed her arm softly to hold her back. "No, wait. Listen."

"*5434968117,*" Olio spoke again, so quickly that the short current of numbers seemed a single word of a strange, indecipherable language.

"Are you alright, Olio?" Adelene shook Etienne's hand away and moved closer.

"5434968117," repeated the android, his voice normal again. He looked up at them from the shadow and seemed to smile. "Those are the first ten digits."

"First ten digits?"

"Yes. Of the code."

29 FOG

Etienne paced back and forth across the tiny room abstractedly. "Ten digits. At least we got *that* far. How many in all? Twelve thousand?"

"I'm not sure."

Etienne chucked halfheartedly.

"So it's a sequence of numbers," Adelene said, fingering a piece of charred wood. "Can you repeat the ones you know?" She touched the carbonized shard to the floor and sketched out the numbers in flaky black marks.

5434968117

Henry came to sniff the markings with curiosity, then grunted and crouched down in a corner by the fire. When she had finished Adelene looked up. "Are you sure you can't remember any more?"

"I'm sorry," Olio whispered, shaking his head.

"It's like they've completely erased that part of his memory," Etienne said, "It's surprising enough that he knows this much despite the reprogramming. I'm starting to think your little robot's got something special to him."

"But how can ten digits help us in any way?"

"I don't know. I'm thinking."

A little whimper escaped Lành's lips in his sleep. Adelene kissed his cheek and stared blankly into the fireplace and its flecks of reddened ash. The disheveled paper pages that had once been laying there were gone, but her mind was too absent to notice. Suddenly an idea struck her and she gasped. "Hacker!"

"What's that?"

'Hacker must know! Olio, call Sara and Hacker and tell them to get over here now. Tell them it's an emergency."

Olio nodded compliantly and obeyed.

"Hacker? That's someone's name?"

"It's what we call him. His real name's Liam Crossrow. He can hack into any computerized system you show him. Trust me. He's gotten into government files before. Maybe he can do something with those ten digits."

"Whoa—Wait. What kind of government files?"

"Files not even the Privileged have access to."

Etienne grinned, his lips still slightly parted in disbelief. "No way." He touched his muscular hand to his forehead and stared out in front of him somewhere between the door and the window, at nothing, and yet at everything. "You know, we might actually pull this through." He looked at Adelene with the same grin still on his face. "This could work!"

Just as he spoke a tumbling sound came from behind the wooden wall. Henry growled.

"Did you hear that?" Adelene whispered. Etienne put his finger to his lips and listened, his somber face blurred in the semidarkness. The fire was out. Henry's ears were perked up and his eyes were fixed on the door again.

"I think someone else is out there." Adelene whispered anxiously.

"I'll go find out." Etienne said, heading towards the

door, pulling his gun from the back pocket of his jeans. He disappeared before he could catch Adelene's anxious whisper calling him back. Henry tried to follow him but the door slammed shut.

The commotion outside made Adelene jump. Her eyes dashed nervously across the room and she squeezed her brother's hand. Lành's whimpering had turned into a low tune, a melody the children sang at school. He hummed it in his sleep. Olio placed his hand comfortingly on Adelene's shoulder. She heard Etienne's voice—harsh, commanding—then another voice answer it in a pathetic cry. She rushed out the door and nearly tripped as she swooped around the corner of the shed, Henry scampering at her side.

Etienne held Sylvan by the collar of his long black coat, both hands clenched angrily around the fine fabric. The frightened boy stared back at him with wide, panicked eyes, his hands stiff along his sides. "Spying on us, buddy?" Etienne spat, his well-defined features obstructed by the shadows of his furrowed brow, "Is that what you're doing? Answer me when I'm talking to you!"

"Etienne!" Adelene yelled. "Stop it! Let him go! I know him!"

Etienne released his grip. "He was spying on us!"

"Sylvan, what are you doing here?"

Sylvan shrunk to the floor and with trembling hands gathered his bee jar and his book and the large black bag next to it. Then he staggered back up on skimpy legs and looked at Adelene, his face a powdery white against the cloudy blackness of the night. "Hi," he said tensely.

"You O.K?" she asked. Henry wobbled over to him and sniffed his shoes. "Come inside. Come. The dog won't hurt you." He did not budge. Adelene sighed and walked up to him. "It's O.K, Sylvan. It was a misunderstanding. We're not mad at you."

"Misunderstanding?" Etienne grimaced. "Misunderstanding—I saw him! He sat there crouched against the wall! Probably hoping to report what he heard."

Adelene threw him a stinging glance over her shoulder as she passed the door. "You too, Etienne. Come back inside, before you wake up the whole ship."

Etienne sighed and followed her without a word. Lành's feeble voice sounded from inside the shed. He still lay asleep on the blanket, his lips moving slightly. Adelene thought she caught a word or two from a song she knew well. A song Myrna used to sing him when he went to bed. A lullaby.

Little child among the stars
Listen to my lullaby...

Olio was watching over him. He had revived the fire, and a flickering yellow light emanated from the fireplace and stretched across the wooden flooring. When he heard them come in he looked up. Sylvan threw a quick glance in the android's direction, then stepped bashfully across the room to his corner by the shelf, and sat down in cagy silence.

"What were you doing, hiding out there by yourself?"

"I came here because I couldn't sleep."

"You came all the way here because—because you couldn't *sleep?*"

"Yes." His fingers tugged at the worn corners of his book. "I don't like sleeping in my house. So I come here."

Adelene sighed. She could see Etienne from the corner of her eye, standing next to her. He let her speak. "And why were you hiding?"

"I thought I was alone and then I heard voices. I didn't know it was you." He pointed at Etienne. "I saw *him*. I don't know who that is."

"This is Etienne. He's with us."

He shook his head. "I don't like him."

"Look, Steven—Sylvan—I'm sorry. It was a mistake, Adelene's right. I thought you were—I didn't know—"

"And who's *he*?"

"That's Lành, my little brother."

"Is he hurt?"

"No, he's fine, although the Police would probably have harmed him if Olio hadn't been there to save him. They're after us. The Authorities. Both of us, and…" Her voice trailed off. Her thoughts turned to fog. Dark fog, impenetrable fog, suffocating, ominous.

"And what?"

"And we have to leave." By her side Lành slept on, whispering the lullaby.

…Thoughts of our world free from wars
Settle in your restful eyes…

"To go where?" Sylvan asked bluntly.

His question hung in Adelene's head for a while and it was hard to formulate an answer. To go where? Earth? Where is Earth? How far is Earth? "Far away." She blurted out. "We have to go very far away. Where nobody can catch us. We have to leave the ship." She felt her mind clog up with fog. She lowered herself onto the cold floor and sat next to her brother again, the moist palms of her hands shaking and the dark mist clouding her vision.

…Sleep until the Lights come back
And the morning of another day
Bears the scent of sweet lilac
Closer to the World Away.

The fog thickened so she felt she couldn't breath

through it, till she couldn't see anything but a little blue planet, blue as Myrna's eye, right in the middle of that fog. Foreign. Distant. A question. A frightening question. *What is Earth?*

30 BOOKMARK

One o'clock.

Sara and Hacker walked at a quick pace up the slope, concealed in the darkness until their silhouettes materialized in the low light that diffused from the shed. Drowsiness still hung in their eyes but they seemed alert. When Sara saw Henry wobble up to her she grinned and peered into the shed.

"Well, hello," Sara said, "Look who finally decided to change his mind! It's our friend Rhynes." Etienne's head jerked up, and when he saw her he tried to say something but she continued, "So what's all this about, Adelene? We both got a call from your buddy here telling us to come as fast as we could. Guess you managed to get the little golem back after all. Is that why you woke us up?"

The way her wavy hair looked in the firelight and the way her eyes captured the darkness in their hazel hue, she was as beautiful as the green-eyed girls of the Centrum Solis. The thought of that evening haunted Adelene's mind. "I'm leaving the ship, Sara."

"You're doing what?" She sniggered, as if it were all one big prank. When Adelene did not smile in return, Sara composed herself and stared at her skeptically.

"Hacker, you said it was possible to leave the ship and you were right. We found a way, and we have to do whatever it takes to make it work. But we need your help. We have this code—"

"Whoa, whoa, calm down," he said, pressing a hand on his forehead as if she were giving him a headache, "Calm down. What are you talking about?"

"Lành and I aren't safe anywhere anymore. I caught Myrna cloning my mother's voice into that hologram Lành keeps on his desk. It was the middle of the night and she should've been deactivated. That's how I found out that the business trip was a lie. My mother's been Detained just like my father."

"Like your father?"

Adelene nodded. "He was Detained for sedition, and my mother kept it from us all these years. Now she's gone too and I have no idea why."

"Myrna told you all of this?"

"No, but I'm sure of it now. I commanded her to tell me the truth, but instead she leaped at me and immobilized me, telling me that if I denied her authority, I denied the Onweald's. At that moment Olio broke into the house through the window and knocked her down. He had been captured, and released with a tracker on his back. He said the Police Droids were coming, and told me to run away and hide." She had left her brother behind. Without omitting a single detail, she described the pursuit with Myrna, and how Etienne had saved her.

"Myrna tried to *kill* you?"

"Yes. And if it weren't for Olio, the Authorities would've taken Lành. Olio saved him from the Police Droids and brought him here. But it won't be long before They find us. And there's worse… I know what happens to the girls who disappear. Like Emmeline."

"Emmeline?" Sara exclaimed, "You know where Emmeline is?"

Adelene cast her eyes down. "I've seen her. Abebi and I have. She's a private prisoner of the Onweald's. Along with other girls." She glanced at Lành from the corner of her eye, then stepped closer to Sara and muttered, "You were right all along, Sara. There are horrible, horrible things happening on this ship. What if my parents are dead? What if They killed them?"

"Don't say that…"

"Myrna would've killed me, Sara. She would've killed me! Who knows what happens to the Detained? I'm all Lành has left to care for him. If I want to protect us both, I can't let the Authorities take me away from my brother the way they took my parents away from us. Olio says we have no choice…"

"Are you saying you want to go back to Earth?"

She took a deep breath. "Yes."

"Tonight?"

"As soon as possible. And whoever wants to come with us is welcome to. If my parents are still alive, we'll come back and save them. We'll find help."

Hacker sighed and walked up to her and spoke more softly. "Adelene, I think there's one thing you don't understand. If you decide to go back, do you even know what you'd be going back to? What if you arrive and realize that the entire human race has wiped itself out? From what we're told, our parents left a planet torn by war, famine and chaos."

"From what we're told, yes," Etienne stated suddenly, "but I don't think They tell us the truth."

"But we can't take such a risk."

The fog was coming again. A fog of fear and questions. Adelene heard Olio's words again. *Leave the ship, you and your brother—Listen to me!—It's the only way.* She could hear her father speaking through him, through the secret guardian who had, for so many years, protected her and Lành. *Trust me, Adelene*, her father's voice said, deep in her mind. He would never let her go back to a rotting Earth. If Olio says it's the way, then it must be the right way.

Adelene gently took Hacker's hand off her shoulder. "I'm leaving, Hacker," she said firmly, "I'm leaving this ship with Lành, and I'm doing it with or without your help."

Hacker sighed and glanced back at Sara, who watched them motionless with her arms crossed. She grinned at Adelene and said, "I'm in. And if we manage to make this work, I'm coming with you."

Adelene stood up and hugged her. She tried to hold back her tears. "Thank you, Sara."

"O.K, Addie, let me go—I can't breath, you're squeezing me so hard."

Hacker gave an acquiescent nod. "Alright, alright. What do you want me to do?"

Adelene showed him the code numbers scribbled on the floor. She explained that they needed to find a way to shut down the entire Security System of the ship—or at least part of it—and that through Olio they had obtained the first ten digits of the control center's access code, but not more. Hacker sat at his computer at the low wooden table, taking in what she told him and thinking.

"Is there anything you can do with that?" Etienne asked.

"It's not going to be easy. Not without knowing the rest of the numbers, or at least how many digits the code is composed of."

Etienne sighed. No one said a word. Adelene stroked Henry who lay flopped down on his side by Lành's blanket with his eyes closed. Even Lành was quiet as he slept. It was so quiet they could almost hear Sylvan's bee buzzing in its jar in the black bag, tapping the glass, looking for a way out. Sylvan sat there quietly with his book in his hands, and that bookmark—the piece of paper with its meaningless scribbles—crumpled between the pages.

Adelene squinted at the bookmark. Tiny numbers, one after the other, orderly, neat, random, smudged and blurred under many greyish fingerprints left by Sylvan's hands. "Sylvan," she mumbled. He looked up, and she moved her arm towards him. "Can I see your bookmark for a second?"

"No," he said harshly, sliding the paper in his coat pocket, "It's mine."

"I know its yours. I'm not going to take it from you. I just want to see what it says."

"It does not say anything. It is just numbers. Numbers and numbers and numbers. My father gave it to me. He says I should never lose it and never give it to anyone."

"Why is it so important?"

All eyes were fixed onto him now. He folded himself into a tiny ball with his shoulders hunched like a protective shield against the many eyes staring at him, as if the eyes were stinging darts thrown at him from all directions. "My father says it's a code to open all doors. That's what he says—my father says—and that's why he gave it to me. He says it is to make sure I am safe in case things go wrong. He's scared, sometimes—my father is. I don't know what it is he's scared of."

"Well then, we won't take it from you. But can you read the numbers to us?" Adelene asked with a patient voice.

A distrustful frown obscured his eyes, but slowly he took the piece of paper back out and slowly read the numbers aloud. "54349681176—"

"That's it!" Adelene squealed, her face beaming with a smile as wide as her astonishment. "The code! Hacker, he's got the code! That's it, isn't it, Olio?"

The little group crowded around Sylvan and stared down

at the piece of paper. Adelene held out her hand and pleaded him to give it to her, just for a little while. He refused again but she insisted, until reluctantly the pale hand with the paper moved up to meet hers. She thanked him, promised she'd return it, and handed it to Hacker.

"Is this really it?" Hacker asked hesitantly, staring at the numbers scribbled on the bookmark.

Adelene nodded. "His father is General Ryffrith, Hacker."

"What?"

"The Minister of Navigation."

"Yes, I know who Ryffrith is! That's *insane!* How do you know this?"

"I saw him, and I had met him before, long ago. These numbers matches up perfectly to the numbers Olio gave us. I'm certain this is what we're looking for."

Hacker sighed and took the bookmark. "Alright. I guess we'll see soon enough." They watched him as he sat there, concentrated on the computer. They watched the screen, too, but what he did made no sense to them. They watched like little children tacitly observing a learned fisherman luring fish. But Hacker furrowed his eyebrows slightly. Something was troubling him.

"Are you getting anything?" Sara asked.

"Hold on—Hold on—I can't…"

"You can't what?"

"It's—I'm—Apparently it's blocking me from getting through."

Etienne stepped in front of Adelene to get a clearer view of the screen. He wanted to help but, by the way he stared at it, it was obvious that Hacker's work made no sense to him either. "Are you sure you entered the code correctly?" he stammered.

"I'm sure. The computer scanned it through. But we've still got a problem. The system's too clever. It's like… It's like it knows I'm not—"

"Not what?" Sara asked impatiently, "Will you *please* communicate, Hacker! We have no idea what you're talking about and you're leaving us hanging here!"

Hacker's eyes popped wide open. "Holy sh—" In one quick move he shut down the computer entirely and fumbled around to make sure nothing was still on.

"What's going on?" Adelene asked in a puzzled tone.

"Check that the signal's dead, Adelene. Right there. That switch there. The red one. Yeah. Hit that. Make sure it stays off."

"What happened?" Sara scowled, "Why'd you stop?"

"Once the code was in, the system somehow identified me as 'non-self.' Then it tried to find my location, so I shut it down as fast as I could. Hopefully I was quick enough."

"It's the DNARS." Sylvan said from his corner.

"The what?"

"The DNA Recognition System."

Once more all eyes were fixed on him, shocked faces, caught by surprise by his sudden interfering. "What's that you're mumbling back there, Bee-man?" Hacker asked.

Sylvan stood up confidently and continued, "The DNARS. It's a Secondary Security System. My father told me about it. Every computer on this ship has this Recognition System on its keyboard. It is there to make sure habitants don't access the type of files and monitors you're trying to access here. Only the Authorities can, along with the Onweald's most high-ranking officers, and His Excellency Himself. Androids don't have DNA. All they need is the code and they are automatically recognized as 'self' by the computer. The Authorities are an integral part of the system itself. *You* aren't."

When Sylvan closed his mouth it was so silent in the shed that one could have heard a pin drop. Time seemed as motionless as the shadows out there in the dark silence of the night, although surely it still crept along. Sara stared at the boy with her arms crossed and her eyebrows raised in disbelief. The same look was echoed on Hacker's face. Incredulity had left them all dumbstruck. Then when the silence had gone on for too long and it was certain Sylvan had said all he had to say, Hacker and Sara looked at each other.

"Well, then," Hacker said, "I think we've misjudged our Bee-man."

31 VERDICT

The long corridor in Hacker's house ended at the door of a small room, hazy in the darkness. It was almost 2:30AM. His parents and his little sister were asleep, and silence reigned in the house. The floorboards creaked under his steps, while Sara walked so furtively and made so little noise that Hacker sometimes looked back to make sure she was still following him. They had gotten in through the open window of his room, so as to not activate Magnus or any of the Service Robots downstairs. Hacker opened the door without a sound and motioned Sara to come along. The door closed softly behind them The room was a study. There was a desk in a corner and a shelf with family pictures. There were other things too, probably decorative objects, but the darkness had blurred these to powdery shadows.

"Hold this," he whispered, handing her Sylvan's bag. The glow of the flashlight fell onto the shelf. He grabbed the sides of the shelf and grunted as he pulled it laboriously away from the wall.

"It's under *there?*"

"Yes," he answered, letting go of the shelf with a strong

exhale and crouching down on his knees. "Right here." He passed his hands along the floorboards until his fingers caught an edge and he pulled.

"Do you need help?" Sara asked.

"Grab that side, if you can."

Sara crouched down at his side and tugged at the loose floorboard. With one last yank the two of them lifted the wooden slate off the ground and laid it quietly aside. Sara flashed the orb of light into the hole and onto the flat, grey object. There was a single symbol on its glossy surface—an apple. "That's a computer?" Sara sneered, "That does *not* look like a computer."

"I know, it doesn't," Hacker chuckled, carefully taking the dusty grey mass out of its hiding place, "but it is. This beauty, my friend, is my great-great grandfather's Macintosh computer from 2014. It hasn't been turned on in decades, and it's been hiding in here since the Departure. My father had it hidden in there all these years just as a keepsake of his grandfather. He knew the Authorities would've insisted on taking it away, but I don't think he had any idea why. This thing's exactly what we need."

"Are you sure this is going to work?"

"Let's hope it does," he replied casually, holding up a fuel cell between his fingers. "If we can get it functioning again we're good. Remember what Bee-man said: All computers manufactured on this ship are equipped with the DNARS. That means every single personal computer in every household of every Division has got it—except for this baby here." He tapped the old Mac's smooth aluminum surface, and the corners of his mouth curved into a sly smile. Then he slipped the computer into the bag and stood up.

"Once we're back outside, I want you to contact Beb and Lily," Sara whispered, "Adelene won't want to leave without saying goodbye to them, and anyway we can't leave

165

them out of this. Tell them to meet us in the Twenty-First. And don't mention the barn, in case the call gets intercepted." Hacker nodded, and the two of them slipped back out of the house the way they had come, quietly and unnoticed. They made their way towards the two lampposts that shone along the mouth of the metro station.

Without Sara and Hacker, the shack felt empty again. In the dead of night there was nothing to disturb the silence save the hums of the night birds and the faint wail of the wind slithering along the wooden planks in the walls.

Lành stirred on the blanket. Etienne took it by the corners and flipped them gently over him. The little hand unconsciously grabbed onto the folded sheet and turned on his side, his feet tucked under him and his body huddled into a little ball. He seemed to be dreaming. He murmured something again. He wasn't humming. Simply murmuring words. Adelene recognized it. So did Etienne, and maybe so did Sylvan, sitting there in his corner. It was the Anthem.

Sing with me the song of our great leader
Of He who guides us with iron courage
And harbors here the children of honor…

"Is he still asleep?" Olio asked.

"I think so," Adelene answered, "I think what happened was difficult for him to bear. He seems a bit fretful. It's not like him to talk in his sleep like that."

"Try not to wake him," Etienne said, "It's best that he stay asleep."

Adelene nodded. The owl hooted somewhere in the trees. A twig snapped in the fire. They barely talked. Adelene came to sit next to Etienne against the shelf. "Thank you for helping us," she said with a smile.

He shook his head. "Nah," he said, "You're helping *me.*"

There were voice outside and Henry's ears perked up again, but this time he was wagging his tail. Sara walked in and Hacker came in after her, carrying the funny grey object and smiling. "We found it!" he said. Lily and Abebi's tired faces materialized behind them.

"Lily! Beb! You're here!" Adelene walked up to them and hugged them. She tried to explain what had happened, but they stopped her.

"We know," Abebi said, "Hacker and Sara told us. Are you alright?"

"I'm fine."

"And Lành?"

"He's sleeping."

They laid the computer on the table and flipped it open.

"How are you going to turn it on?" Lily asked.

Hacker took the fuel cell from his pocket. "Let's hope they had *these* back in 2014."

They grouped around him again and watched him pull out a screwdriver from his bag, like the ones in old movies, and unscrew the little square flap under the computer and tweak things around a little, and fumble with the tiny cables, and insert the fuel cell carefully like he had been doing this his whole life. Then he carefully put everything back together and breathed in deeply and pressed the tiny *on* button. Everyone held their breath. Hacker kept the button pressed down and mumbled, "Come on, come on…"

The screen flickered. The dusty old thing made a noise and the screen turned on for good. Bright, two-dimensional pixels coming back to life. They all whooped and shouted and tapped Hacker amicably on the shoulder as he stared at the computer screen with a big smile. It was a strange feeling they all felt, knowing that the last time this tattered old apparatus had been turned on was when no one had set foot in the *Inceptum Fidelis* yet, when it was still being constructed up above planet Mars, or not even started at all. It was strange to think that nothing of the world they knew existed back then. Light years separated this little grey object's world from theirs—Light years, an untold history and a different future, like in a parallel universe—And that was the world Adelene, Sara and Lành were going back to on that escape vessel.

"Someone pass me the code again," Hacker said, "I need to get this thing to establish a signal. Connect it to the ship's system, somehow."

The rest of them watched him work with baffled faces again. They watched him talk half to himself as the tips of his fingers tapped the keys on the keyboard. Their eyes followed the little black arrow on the screen that he seemed to control. Hacker turned to Olio and told him he had him connected to the computer, and needed him to scan the code. Olio obeyed and the numbers of the code formed onto the screen. "Guys, I can't do this with so many people crowding around me," Hacker said, taking his hands off the keyboard with nervous irritation, "So unless you think you can help in any way, just give me some space, ok?"

Everyone backed away without a word. Adelene went back to where Lành slept on and stroked his hair again. Sara crossed her arms and wandered up to the shelf. She picked up a book. Just before opening it she looked at Etienne from the opposite side of the room and made sure his eyes met hers, then waved the book at him with a shrewd smile. *You didn't burn this one*, her eyes said. She leaned against the wall and flipped through the pages.

Etienne looked down at his feet, his hands in his pocket. Without realizing it, he lifted a hand to touch his cheek where she had kissed him, but when he looked back up and saw that she was still looking at him, he passed the gesture off as simply scratching at his stubble. She tried to conceal a small smile and stared down at her book. She wasn't really reading.

"Guy, guys—I—I've found—I've found a path!" The abrupt sound of Hacker's voice made them all look up again and got them jumping back to their feet. "Yes!" Hacker called out, "I got it! Ha! I got it! Look at this!" They peered down at the screen. Sylvan stood there too, quietly looking down at the two-dimensional array of files, words, images and sounds.

"You did it!" Abebi squealed.

Hacker laughed, "Ladies and gen'lmen, I present to you"—and he leaned back with a proud grin, almost forgetting he was in a stool—"the most confidential archives of the Inceptum Fidelis, right here, dating back to the Departure."

"This is *insane*!" Sara chuckled, staring at the screen in awe.

Hacker tapped the edge of the computer again. "The crappy old thing had it in 'im after all! Look, look, look! What's this?" He enlarged an image on the screen, a blurred shot of the Onweald in his lavish quarters at the helm of the ship. Standing by him were Gold Star officers sealed tightly into neat grey uniforms, and two or three Admirals with spotless white bodies and gold-plated joints.

"It looks like some kind of recording," Adelene said.

"*June 15, 2114*," Lily mumbled, "That date sounds familiar."

"Where?"

"Right there," she said, pointing to the small red numbers at the bottom of the image.

"The communication cut-off," Etienne said, stepping in confidently, "June 2114, that was the date of the communication cut-off, eleven years ago."

"He's right," Hacker said, "That's the date we lost communication with the planet. The initial prediction was something like 2159. Then, six years into the voyage, bam! Bad news, ladies and gen'lmen, communication's gone."

Adelene looked at him with puzzled eyes. "So that means—"

"It *means* that this, here, is footage of the last exchange between the ship and the Earth."

The image wheezed and rattled and shook as the old computer strained to interpret the data, and then the Onweald's face became clear. He looked only slightly younger than he did now, his skin less grey and his hair somewhat darker, and only stubble where his moustache now showed. The officer at the large control deck, spread out in a hexagonal shape across the room, said something to him. At first the voice was raspy and broken, but slowly the sound became clearer.

'A signal from Earth, your Excellency," the officer said. The Onweald stepped towards the deck with his hands locked together behind his back and a cold look in his eyes, as constricted as his posture.

A grainy voice rose from the black device among the controls and holograms that protuberated from the center of the deck. *This is the Deep Space Network of the United States NASA. We contact you to inform you with great contentment that the war is over, and that in recent years our Administration has tested, and is now in the process of assembling, a new spacecraft, Project X9-Agathon, which will make the same voyage you are undertaking, but in less than 30 years.* The Onweald stepped closer with the same stony look. He listened. The voice spoke on: *The President therefore entreaties a cancellation of the mission Inceptum Fidelis, as a multi-generational expedition is no longer necessary. We eagerly wait to welcome home your courageous crew. All 300,000 passengers will be greatly compensated upon your return. This is doubtless grand news for you as well, and even more so for those of the middle generation, who shall thereby no longer expect to live out their lives on the ship."*

The officers waited for him to respond, but the Onweald stood still.

They waited for an order, but he gave none.

"Inceptum Fidelis, do you copy? The voice sounded again. *Inceptum Fidelis, I repeat, it is with great joy that we inform you that you may turn your ship around and head for home, for we have made extensive progress since your departure, and are launching a new mission that—"*

That's when he did it. They saw that great iron hand clamp down onto the device and yank it out of its socket, and heard the voice twist and contort and fade out into blotted, fragmented noise.

The Onweald made a slight gesture of the hand towards the Admirals. They nodded their rigid robotic heads obediently, and that was when the words appeared on the large grey screen: *Mayday. Mayday.*

"Is that—?" Abebi's voice rose up shyly, as if she were afraid to break the eerie silence that had taken over them all as they stood gathered around the grainy videotape.

"The distress signal," Hacker mumbled. He placed his elbow on the edge of the table and covered his mouth with his hand, anxiously. "I—I don't understand."

The officer by the Onweald's side turned his head slowly to meet the cold eyes, his dry lips slightly parted in astonishment. The officer tried to remain composed, but the look in his eyes and the oily shine of perspiration on his brow betrayed his alarm, his panic.

The image froze, and turned black. No one said a word. Hacker must have touched key on the keyboard, for then the files on the screen began to move and change. Words and numbers flashed in green and black as the old computer struggled to recapture the connection signal, and then a green radar materialized, beeping as circles of green light rippled from a red point at it center.

"What is that?" Adelene asked.

"It's our locator," Etienne answered, "The point in the middle must be the ship, but the scope here is too narrow for us to see any nearby planet or star."

"But if we zoom out a bit," Hacker said, tapping keys on the keyboard again, "to a radius of about... one parsec... we should start to see—"

There it was, the Earth, a small green dot at one extremity of the radar, encased in a blue square displaying its coordinates. Extending from it to the center of the radar was a path—strait at first, and then abruptly curved.

"Why does it curve so much there?" Adelene asked.

"The ship's changing directions. Probably because of some kind of obstacle. Let's zoom out more. Diameter of seven parsecs." At the opposite boundary of the circular monitor appeared another planet, a green dot encased in a square and labeled *Terminus*. "That's our destination. But... this is strange."

"What?" Lily asked.

"The ship seems slightly off course."

All eyes stared at the beeping red point at the center, its path curved westwards on the screen. Hacker tapped keys on the keyboard again and clicked around with his mouse, uttering, *Predicted Path*. In response a dotted line formed past the red dot, extending off into space, farther and farther away from the Terminus. "Holy sh—" Hacker's voice trailed off. The dotted line continued on and on, bending and changing only to avoid collision, until finally neither Earth nor the Terminus were encompassed on the screen. It was all blackness. The red dot beeped and beeped. The dotted line continued on. There was no Terminus.

"This doesn't make sense," Hacker said breathlessly, "We're going nowhere."

"What do you mean?" Abebi asked, almost inaudibly, fear mounting in her voice.

Hacker stopped the dotted line and returned to the initial standpoint. He clicked on the path of the ship, right on the spot where it initially began to curve leftward. Numbers appeared below it. *062114.*

Sara covered her mouth with her hand and mumbled, "June 2114!"

"Oh man," Hacker said with the same incredulity in his voice, "We're not going anywhere."

The truth stabbed them like knives—stung them from inside that little screen—each beep of the radar like a thousand thunderbolts. It bit into their minds and shook them awake. Eleven years ago, Earth had called the ship back. Eleven years ago, the Onweald had cut off communication, erased all trace of the ship's survival, and slowly, silently, shifted its course.

Slowly, silently, the great *Inceptum Fidelis* loomed through the black void, forever sailing into soundless, massless, airless space, into oblivion. There was no turning back, and there would be no arriving. Thus had been the verdict for eleven years.

We're not going anywhere.

32 ABSCOND

"All of us. This is our only chance. We go back and get help."

"But, Sara, this could be dangerous!"

"We don't have a choice, Lily! You've seen the radar. The ship's going *nowhere*. The Onweald's changed the course because he didn't *want* to turn back—Why? Because he's very happy here with his concubines and his palace—and here we are ignorantly drifting towards *nothing!* What do you think will happen in 200 years, when the food supply runs out? When there's nowhere to turn to for help? When the Onweald couldn't care less about his people because he'll be stone dead in his florid tomb! What then?"

No one answered her. The little boy stirred in his sleep.

"We have to do something and this is our chance!" Sara took Adelene's arm. "I'm leaving with Adelene, and whoever wants to come with us has to speak up now."

"I'm coming," Hacker said, standing up confidently, "I was planning on coming anyway." He smiled, and Adelene smiled back.

"Me too," Etienne said, "What kind of morons would we be to let you two girls go off into Space by yourselves?"

A warmth spread through Adelene like a little candle lighting up inside of her. She wasn't alone anymore. She had never been alone. She caught a smile on Sara's face. A small smile, but a real one nonetheless.

Sylvan quietly pulled himself to his feet and stepping towards Adelene. He stood by her side and looked at the others, clutching the bee jar in his hand. He held out his hand towards Abebi and Lily, who sat huddled together by the fire. "Come on," he said, and leaned in to take Abebi's hand and pull her up.

Lily hesitated, stroking Bear who lay curled up in the palms of her hands, then stood up as well. "Screwed if you do, and screwed if you don't," she sighed. She pushed a loose strand of her short brown hair from her face, crossed her arms, and smiled at Adelene. "Let's get out of here."

"We've got about two hours before daylight," Hacker said, his voice catching back its pressing seriousness, "I'm going to transfer these data files and codes onto Olio. He can then shut down the Central Security System himself. Sending the signal from a versatile android registered as *Self* by the system is much safer and will save us time."

"We can't waste time," Etienne said, "Everyone gather up their things and take out your contact lenses if you've got them on." He walked over to where Lành lay asleep and gently lifted him in his arms. The little boy groaned feebly, then slightly opened his eyes.

"Where are we?" he asked in a small voice. There were dark circles under his eyes and his face was pale in the light of the fire.

Adelene kissed his cheek. "You're safe now, Lành. I'm here. We're going away on a rocket ship."

"A rocket ship?"

Etienne propped him up on his back. "Wrap your arms around my neck, buddy. I'm going to carry you, alright? Don't let go."

"We're going on a rocket ship?"

"Yes, a rocket ship," Adelene said softly, "It's a ship that Daddy wanted us to take. And it's going to take us back to Earth."

"What about Mommy?"

"We'll come back for Mommy later, Lành."

"But I want to stay here," he whispered, "I want to stay *here*…" And he dosed off into sleep again.

Hacker closed the computer and stuffed it back in Sylvan's bag. "Done," he said. "Everything transferred properly. Olio, once we get to Flemington, I'll give you a signal. You've got to shut down everything. I want every single microbot in the entire Twenty-Ninth Division deactivated, you understand?"

Olio nodded.

"And how long do we have before They realize that something's interfering with the system?" Sara asked.

"About forty-five minutes. Maybe less. Just make sure no one keeps his or her lenses on."

"But I'm near-sighted," Abebi said.

"You're going to have to get rid of the glasses anyway, Beb. I'm sorry. We just can't risk detection."

Abebi sighed, and then dispassionately threw her glasses into the fire. She squinted as her eyes struggled to adjust to the blurry world.

"Can you see alright?" Lily asked, concerned.

"Yeah, I'll be fine. Just don't go too far ahead of me."

"What about the dog?" Adelene asked, "All pets have trackers."

"Then we'll have to leave him here," Hacker said, "I'm sorry, Etienne."

Etienne nodded. "No, I understand. That's the best thing to do." The commotion had woken Henry up as well and the dog stood at his master's feet, panting happily.

Abebi adjusted the scarf around her neck. "How are we

going to make it to Flemington before dawn? It's eight kilometers from here and the metro's too risky this late at night."

"She's right," Lily said, "They'll stop us and start asking questions. We'll get caught for sure."

"We'll take horses once we get to Anderson," Sara said.

"We can't. Stables are closed at night."

"The fencing is made of wood and it's barely a meter high, Adelene. We'll manage. And if there's a door to get through I'm sure your golem could help us out. Now let's get going. We don't have much time."

They walked out one after the other, quietly, Sylvan carrying his book and the jar with the bumblebee, Etienne carrying Lành on his back. The sky was already lighter, and a low fog had settled like a blanket over the hills and in the trees. Henry followed behind, tail wagging and snout sniffing the ground eagerly.

"No, Henry," Etienne said, "You stay here. Stay." The dog looked up at him, his big wet tongue lolling out. The boy sighed, and gave Lành over to Olio. He led Henry back to the doorstep of the old barn and squatted down in front of him, stroking his shaggy coat. "Sit, Henry. Sit. Good boy! You gotta stay, here, alight? I'll be back soon."

Henry sat on his haunches in the doorway, fidgeting and whimpering like an oversized puppy. Etienne scratched him behind the ear, then stood back up and slowly walked away saying, "Stay… Stay… Good boy, Henry. Stay. Good boy."

Henry obeyed, and watched the little group walk away into the muddled darkness. And even when the night had entirely engulfed them, Etienne could still see him sitting obediently in the light of the doorway, staring into the night.

***

They could hear the horses in the stable whinnying at the

sound of footsteps approaching. Under the grey glow of the streetlights the stable and the houses and the trees were grey and spectral. Hacker jumped quietly over the fence and stole across the paddock. He stopped at the tall entrance of the stable and motioned the rest of them to do the same. One by one they joined him, gently carrying Lành over and passing the black bag from one person to the next, until all eight of them stood huddled by Hacker's side.

"How do we get in?" Abebi whispered.

"Break through."

"What?"

"Well it's not like They've got whole alarm systems with special lasers installed in there. No one *steals* horses, Beb."

Olio broke through the large doors with little effort, slamming his foot against the slit between them until the hinges twisted and gave way. Along the cold flooring inside, startled shadows neighed and whinnied and hooves pounded against the ground. The air had the dry, dusty smell of hay and cattle. They untied five horses and saddled them, and then led them outside one after the other, calming them with soft words and caresses.

A loud, confused voice sounded from somewhere nearby, and without wasting another minute they mounted the horses. Olio threw himself against the wooden fence, letting it crash down into the moist earth, and led the horses through. Adelene sat behind Sara on a lean black mare and looked back over her shoulder to check on her brother. Lành's eyes were open again, and they seemed creased by dark circles against his pallid features. "I'm tired," she thought she heard him say in a small voice, "Where are we going?"

She watched Olio heave the boy up onto Etienne's horse, then jump swiftly onto his own saddle. Atop the horse, Olio's slender silhouette looked exceedingly human. Following them were Sylvan and Abebi on a grey speckled horse. Lily rode behind Hacker at the front of the group and held Bear gently against her chest with one hand.

They reached the road, and Adelene squeezed her eyes shut as Sara brought the horse to a gallop. "Seven kilometers to Flemington," Sara called out to the others as they passed under the southern outlet, "You think we can make it?"

"Of course we can!" Hacker shouted over his shoulder. As the hooves clobbered against the road faster and faster, Adelene felt the wind blow against her face and lift her hair into the air. The corners of her lips curled into a secret smile. She felt happy. Free.

She watched the villages pass along the road, one Division after the other, small houses neatly aligned beside tidy gardens and pools. It was not long before they reached Middleton. Etienne raised one hand up silently, motioning them to slow down. "We can't be seen here," he said as quietly as he could.

"Etienne's right. The Police Droids were here only a couple of hours ago." Hacker curbed his horse and turned to the others. "They might still be roaming around. We'll go through the forest paths and rejoin the main road once we're closer to the outlet on the other side of the Division." The horses snorted and grunted and vapor rose in clouds from their warm muzzles. Adelene passed her eyes one last time over the little pond by her own home, tracing the way to the front door with her eyes. One last time, before disappearing among the trees.

Four o'clock. It was colder now. The mist rose higher and higher as the night dissipated slowly around them. So early in the morning Flemington was a ghost town. The narrow streets were silent. The tall houses and their long shadows were silent. The great metropolis of hearsay and idle talk had closed its immense mouth and gone to sleep. One bird chirped in the hazy trees by the chapel. The

Ceiling, like silent shutters, had begun to close. Soon the Lights would shine into morning and the habitants would wake, and go about the daily simplicity and calm of their lives. And once more the mouths would tell the stories they had dreamed and heard and judged, till finally their minds would be so full of each other's stories, and reality so tangled up and mashed together, that words would replace their lives.

"Now, Olio," Hacker whispered with a small gesture of his hand towards the robot.

Olio nodded. He froze abruptly, staring into space and mumbling something incomprehensible, mechanical as a talking puppet. All eyes were fixed onto him, waiting in anxious silence. Then he jumped off his horse and told them that it was done. The system was shut down, and they must follow him now.

"It's this way," Olio said, pointing towards the West Wall that rose up to meet the Ceiling, far behind the buildings.

They left the horses near a bridge along the bank of a watercourse, where, between the round cobblestones, several patches of grass and dandelions grew. "I'm sure a Service Robot will see them there and bring them back," Sara said offhandedly.

The group made its way along the sidewalks of the shadowy streets, quietly following Olio and Adelene. Once in a while Olio would turn around and wave them forward saying, "This way, this way." His eyes beamed a gentle blue light.

They stumbled into a dark alley that ended at the foot of the West Wall. The street looked uneven and torn, as though the dark buildings leaning on either side of the it had squeezed tighter and tighter around it with the passing of the years. There were neglected composite bins along the walls, and the only light came from a faint yellow fog that oozed up from a barred manhole along the narrow, rutted sidewalk.

"People sure don't pass by here very often," Hacker said.

"That Cleaner there is deactivated." Sylvan pointed to a small, immobile form lying on the ground against a broken container.

"I guess he was part of the Security System as well," said Lily.

Sara sniggered. "Well then, there are more little buggers spying on us than I thought."

"I guess my father was right, you got to watch what you say even when the only one around is your kitchen Cleaner.'

They reached the base of the Wall and Olio mumbled something to himself. He touched his hand to the Wall. "We'll go through here," he said, "This is an entrance."

"How do you know?"

Hacker allowed himself a small laugh. "He's probably got the whole map of the ship stuck in his head right now—ever since I transferred all of the information onto him."

Before anyone could say another word, the Wall produced a series of low beeping noises, followed by quick jolts like a turning lock. A slit formed where the facade had until then seemed intact, and part of the Wall sank into the ground like a blade, revealing a low arched corridor. Adelene looked back one last time at the Division.

She looked up at the Ceiling. At the clouds forming below it.

At the Lights.

And then Olio led them into the vaporous obscurity of the passage, his eyes illumining the vaulted metallic walls and the endless maze of shafts, doors and turns. Adelene didn't know who else had looked back one last time. Sara and Etienne had walked into the passage before her, but in their full confidence—or maybe because they had simply forgotten—neither of them had looked back.

Their feet clanked loudly against the steel, and even louder as they stumbled down the steep stairway that sank away into the depths of the ship. Lily's hands trembled as she grasped on to the railing. Hacker took out his flashlight. "It's so dark down here," he grumbled.

"And cold," Lily said.

Sylvan looked around. "Where do we go now, Olio?"

"Through here. Follow me." They sprawled further through the dim corridor, breathless from the weight of their excursion, deaf from the hissing of vapor that exuded from the ground, blind but to the small blue orbs of light from Olio's eyes. Once in a while Adelene would stop and call out, "Lành?"

"I've got him, I've got him," Etienne's voice would answer from somewhere behind her, "Keep moving, we can't stop." Finally the corridor widened and fluorescent beams lined the ceiling, most of them flickering oddly like the wings of dying insects.

Adelene's eyes passed across the ceiling and she murmured, "I recognize this place."

Olio stopped just where she expected. There the passage ended, and there stood the heavy round door squeezed along the wall next to similar dark doors. Olio touched his hand to the door, then smiled. "They never thought of rebuilding a sturdier one." He took a few steps back and smashed through the door. It crashed to the ground with a screeching thud and a gush of cold air washed over them. They peered through the opening at the immensity of the room beyond, and the smooth whiteness of the many spacecrafts aligned along the ground.

They walked in and stared, speechless. Etienne sniggered. "That was too easy."

Among the many vessels Adelene recognized the

Alcubierre ship. "That's it! That's our ship there," she told them. She led them towards it.

"A ship inside a ship," Sara said, looking up in awe.

Just then the barking of a dog echoed out of the passageway. Etienne gave Lành to Olio and listened. The barking grew louder and louder. "Oh no," he muttered, and ran back to the smoky doorway. "Henry?" He called out. "Henry! Over here, buddy!" The big dog materialized from the gaseous obscurity of the passageway and ran up to his master, tail wagging and tongue lolling from the side of his mouth. "How did you get here? How did you find us, bud?" Etienne hugged him and petted the shaggy fur between the dog's floppy ears. "I can't believe this! He followed us all the way here!"

"This is bad," Hacker said, "He's got a tracker, Etienne! He'll reveal our presence here!"

Suddenly a booming sound resounded across the high ceiling. With it the ground seemed to quiver slightly, then all was immobile and silent again. They held their breath. Sara put her finger to her mouth, her eyes moving nervously across the ceiling and the walls, seeking the source of the sound. Henry stopped wagging his tail and whimpered nervously.

"What was that?" Lily whispered.

"I don't know."

Olio plugged his ears with his hands. "The noise…" he whispered, is face clenched in an agonized expression, "Make it stop!"

"What do you hear, Olio?"

"Voices. Orders."

"Orders?"

"We've been detected. They're coming. We have to hurry."

"Everybody board the ship!" Hacker yelled. "Now! Go, go, go!"

The entrance rapidly opened onto the cockpit of the ship and Olio ran up the ramp just as it lowered to the floor. "Come on!" He motioned them with his hand as he stood between the bright entranceway and the ramp. Hacker took Lành inside, then pulled Sara up by the arm and gently led her up the ramp, then turned back around to take Lily's hand.

"Where's Abebi?" Lily called out suddenly just as she placed her foot on the cold metal of the ramp. Panic had washed the color from her face.

"I thought she was with you!" Adelene turned around and dashed back out of the ship. "Etienne! We're missing Beb!"

Etienne looked around. "Abebi!" He called out.

"We lost her! She couldn't see well without her glasses!"

"We have to go back!" Lily cried.

"Abebi!" Etienne called out again. He looked back at Adelene, his eyes wide and dark with alarm. "Get on the ship. I'm going back." Without waiting for a response, he dashed back to the door and disappeared into the passageway with Henry following closely behind.

"Come on, Adelene," Hacker said, extending his hand towards her. She hesitated before entering, looking back through the door where Etienne had disappeared. A low droning reverberated through the wide walls. And then she heard the voices that sent fear crawling into her mind. *Unauthorized Intrusion Alert. Repeat, Detected Intrusion: Section 911482. Alert. Security breach.*

"They're here," she murmured, passing her eyes over the shadowy ceiling far above, seeking out the Droids.

"Get onto the ship!" Olio said, running up to her, "We won't leave without them, I promise!"

Adelene grabbed his hand, her eyes still fixed on the ceiling, and just as she pulled herself up the shadows twisted and stretched into distorted figures. Thousands of red eyes stared down at them from above like an angered beehive. *You stand in Violation of the Law*, the monotonous voices hissed, *Abandon any further Unlawful Stratagem.*

It was like falling into the same nightmare again. The voices coming after her in the dark. The fear. But this time she wasn't alone. This time she felt her friends' arms around her, hands holding hers. They won't let anything harm her just as she won't let anything harm them. Olio ran to the deck at the front of the spacecraft and began to maneuver it, agilely manipulating the controls. The ship rumbled, and they felt it advance slowly under their feet.

Surrender to His Excellency.

The ship moved to the center of the wide path that stretched between the rows of white ships and led to the broad gate beyond.

Concede Immediately or We shall be Forced to take Compulsory Measures to Halt you.

"There he is!" Sylvan yelled, peering out from the open entrance of the ship and pointing towards the passageway, "I see them! It's Etienne! And he's got Abebi with him!"

The two figures darted out of the passageway and ran towards the ship, followed by Henry. Etienne held Abebi by the arm and hurried her on. The young girl's face was washed with tears and her eyes full of fear.

"Help them get on!" Hacker called out.

The Droids had aligned themselves on the parameters of the vast compartment, guns pointed at the ship. There was no order given. The high-pitched gunfire sounded all at once—needles of sound perforating the air.

Abebi screamed and covered her head with her hands. Sara retreated from the open entrance and yelled, "They're shooting at us!"

"Hurry!" Hacker took Abebi's hand and pulled her onto the advancing spacecraft. Henry jumped in after her and remained at the edge of the entrance, yelping. A projectile hissed through the air right above Etienne's head and exploded against the wing of the spacecraft, sending through it a deafening tremor. Adelene caught his hand and heaved him onto the ship, and he collapsed onto the cold flooring.

Lily squeezed Abebi in her arms, crying. "I'm so sorry, Beb! It's all my fault! I should've been watching out for you! I'm so sorry!"

"Alright, we've got everyone! Let's go!" Hacker said, waving his arms at Olio.

The robot nodded and closed the entrance, locking out the gunshots.

Another tremor flung them to the ground. "Get us out of here now or we're all dead!" Lily cried, "The ship's not going to stand any more blows!"

"It's going, it's going!" Olio said. They looked out the wide cockpit window as the furthermost wall of the great expanse tore open like a massive steel door. Behind it appeared the stars, floating in trillions across a boundless, airless abyss.

They felt their small spaceship accelerate towards the open mouth of the black vacuum. They stared wide-eyed at the darkness until it engulfed them.

"Look at it," Lily said quietly, peering through the small, angular windows at the rear of the spacecraft. "It's so… huge."

They watched the gigantic steel monster shrinking away into the distances, its two spectacular wheels spinning slowly around the Axis. Its head, the great Beryllium shield bloated with its supply of water, advanced coldly on.

Suddenly, their escape vessel ceased to accelerate, and seemed to come to a stop. The *Inceptum Fidelis* was still in view, a smudge of meaningless grey matter on a canvas of nihility. "What's happening?" Lily whispered in a fretful, broken voice.

"We've reached a safe distance from the *Inceptum Fidelis* to begin the Alcubierre drive," Olio explained. "In order for the ship to travel faster than light, we are expanding the fabric of space behind the ship and shrinking space-time in front of the ship, creating a kind of 'space bubble.' I only need to authenticate the—"

A sudden tremor shook the ship and an alarm pierced the stillness. ALERT. The word appeared in red on the communication panel in the center of the control deck, flashing and beeping. ALERT.

"Oh no." Olio sighed.

"What was that?" Hacker asked, trying to stay calm.

"We're being followed." The robot touched his hand to the controls on the screen. "No significant damage has been done, but there are five or six Exploration Agents on my radar and—"

"And they're following us?" Abebi cried out.

"More like *shooting* at us!" Sara retorted. The ship shook once more, and the alarm doubled in frequency, in succession with warning flashes of lurid red light. "Listen, whatever the hold-up is, you got to solve it fast or we're all dead!"

"I know! I'm trying, I'm trying! Hold on!"

"One of the shields is gone!" Hacker shouted in panic, running to the front of the ship, "They've hit the shield generator!"

A crushing dizziness weighed down on Adelene's mind. The sound of the alarm was heavy and monotonous. It was overwhelming. She was again the tiny pixel of life, insignificant and defenseless. With one more detonation of their missiles, the Authorities would destroy the fragile little ship. It was simple—so simple. On the little screen in the cockpit the red words appeared: ALERT: *Enemy projectile launched. 8 seconds until impact.*

"Olio, please!"

"I've almost got it! Hold on! 3, 2, 1—"

There came a sonorous boom from all around the small spacecraft. Adelene covered her ears. Henry yelped, and cowered down in a corner with his tail curled back between his legs and his head held low. One loud boom, and the world they knew fell behind. In seconds it was gone. Only when the stress and fear finally dissipated did they realize it, and a chocking anxiety overcame them all. They did not move. They did not speak. They did not look at each other.

A calm, womanly voice echoed smoothly across the walls of the spacecraft. *Initiation successful. Alcubierre drive is now in effect.*

Olio jumped up joyfully. "It worked!" He said, laughing, "It's working!"

"But—It's like we're not moving at all," Etienne said.

"That's normal! The ship isn't actually moving, you see. We're stationary! Or, one could say, in a kind of free-fall. The *Inceptum Fidelis* was powered by antimatter, while our vessel here has been modified to use Exotic Matter, thus allowing it to create the distortion in space that will bring us to our destination at superluminal speeds."

"And you've figured all of that out by yourself?" Etienne smiled. The others stared at him with incomprehensive faces, mystified by that smile. Wasn't he just as petrified as they were? Wasn't he also leaving behind everything he ever knew? There was something about him that they all respected and admired, but they couldn't place a word on what it was. "I guess I was wrong about you," Etienne continued, his smile still there on his lips, "You're much more than a senseless babbler."

For a while all was silent again. Etienne stared out the great window of the cockpit into the blackness, and Sara sat cross-legged in one of the dimly lit walkways across from him, her coat folded under her. Adelene held Lành up against her, with her arms wrapped protectively around his shoulders. He sniveled and mumbled something in a tearful voice. The boy's face was ashen and ghostly under the dim lights, and there were dark circles under his eyes.

"Olio," Adelene said faintly, "I think Lành is sick."

Hacker walked over to where she was sitting and looked down at the sleeping child. "Let him rest a bit," he said coolly, "All this has probably been a bit hard on him. Probably traumatizing for a little kid. I'm sure he'll be better tomorrow."

Tomorrow. The word floated in her mind for a while, looking for a place to settle in. When would tomorrow come? Would it ever come? Did Time exist on this ship? Were they anywhere at all? She kissed Lành's warm cheek and put her ear to his chest, listening to the heartbeat. Then she touched her hand to her own heart. If nothing existed anymore, if there was no way to tell anything had ever existed at all, or if anything was real, then at least she could trust the heartbeats.

33 INDOCTRINATED

Lily sat crouched in a corner. Bear was nestled comfortably in her cupped hands. He licked his paws and rubbed his furry muzzle, then licked them again and passed them behind his ears and on his belly. Sitting back on his haunches, he scratched his side lazily. It was quiet. No one said a word. Suddenly Lily gasped, her eyes fixed on the little hamster. "What's happening?"

"Lily, it's O.K," came Sara's halfhearted answer, "He's just grooming himself."

"I can't feel him!"

"What do you mean?" Sara stood up, caught with sudden curiosity and, though it was in her usual disposition not to show it, concern.

The sudden agitation reached the ears of others, and they came too, to crowd around Lily and stare down at the hamster with astonishment. Bear looked up at her with his large, beady eyes, and stood up on his hind legs. His paws were pressed against his velvety white belly. Gently, she tried to touch the soft brown fur between his ears, but her hand went right through. She gasped and drew her hand back. "What's happening?" She was panicking. Her voice trembled as she spoke. "It's like—It's like I'm holding a ghost!"

Cannot find simulation records.

"Simulation records?" Sara said, reading the words that had materialized in front of the hamster. "Your rat's fake?"

The hamster's figure wavered like a computer image struggling to keep its focus, reappeared again, then disintegrated entirely. Lily stared down at her empty hands. "I don't—I don't understand."

"It's fake! How is that possible?"

"It was a Mimus," Hacker said, "I'm almost sure of it. I've heard of these things. The Askancists claimed that they existed, but I never believed them until now."

"A Mimus?"

"Yes. They're created to simulate certain animals that could pose a threat to the habitants as disease carrying, aggressive, poisonous or whatever else if introduced on the ship. Lily's hamster was therefore a high-technology hologram perceptible by touch, sight and hearing, with the ability to mimic a real rodent's behavior. And apparently it can virtually develop an individual personality to the same degree as a real hamster."

"So now that we're so far from the ship, it can't locate its records. So it can't function anymore. I'm sorry, Lily. I know you held dearly to that hamster."

Lily sighed. "It's alright. I just—" A tear rolled down her cheek. She wiped it away shamefully with her hand. " I just feel so far from home."

Adelene sat next to Lily and laid her head against her shoulder. "It's O.K, Lily," she said quietly, "We all do."

"So, who's next? The dog?" Sara sniggered, turning to Henry, "Are you a fake too? Are you going to crumble away into nothingness as well?" The dog sat on his haunches with a happy smirk on his snout and his ears perked up. He barked at her, delighted at the attention.

Suddenly they heard a scream. Lành lay with his head on Adelene's laps, turning and thrashing about, mumbling inarticulate words. His face was ghostly pale, and his eyes squeezed shut as if in pain.

"Lành? Lành!" Adelene cried, "Wake up, Lành!"

Etienne rushed towards them and kneeled next to Adelene. He touched the boy's forehead with his hand, his eyes dark with concern.

"His forehead's very hot," Adelene said in a trembling voice, "What are we going to do?"

"Calm down, Adelene," Etienne said, gently taking her hand, "He's going to be O.K. We have plenty of medicine on this ship. It's going to be alright."

Lành moaned again, then mumbled something once more. Adelene leaned her ear closer to her brother's lips and said, "What's he saying? Do you understand any of it?"

Etienne motioned her to stop talking and listened to the boy's murmurings. "It's—It's a song."

"What do you mean?"

"He's singing a song. It's in Latin. I know this song." The alarmed look was still anchored on his face. "It's *The Paean*, a song of praise to the Onweald. Why is he singing this?" Suddenly a thought seemed to strike him. Fear caught hold of him.

"What's wrong?" Lily asked.

"Adelene, when the Police Droids broke into your house, did They lay hands on Lành before Olio saved him?"

"Yes, They did, but only briefly. Olio went in and saved him before They could take him away."

Etienne said nothing. Although he tried to hide his unease, they could all see it in his eyes. He tried to gently shake the boy awake but Lành only whimpered weakly. Etienne pulled up the boy's sleeves and looked closely at his forearms.

"What are you doing? Is he O.K.?"

"Help me lift him up. I need to check something."

Without a word Adelene did as he told her. Even pulled upright, Lành did not wake up. "Lành! Lành, honey, it's me! Please wake up."

Etienne pushed the curly auburn hair away from the boy's neck, revealing a tiny metal object extending from beneath the skin just below the boy's left ear. "Just what I thought," he said, panic rising in his voice.

"What is that?" Adelene gasped, "What have they done to him!"

"It's a brainwashing drug released slowly into his bloodstream. It's very dangerous. Someone find me an anesthesia pill! We're going to need to pull this thing out."

"Pull it out?"

"Yes—Or cut it out, if it comes to that. Trust me, Adelene. I know what I'm doing."

"I can't lose him!" Tears rose to Adelene's eyes. "Just tell me he's going to be alright."

"Listen. I'm going to do everything I can. It's only been a few hours. If we take it out now he'll be alright. I promise. But we can't afford to wait any longer."

She looked up at him with distressed eyes, and then nodded meekly.

They laid Lành on a blanket and Olio came up to them with a small white pill and a glass of water. Lành was calm again, and his eyes were slightly opened. He looked up at his sister and tried to say something.

"Raise his head a little," the robot said. He dissolved the pill in the water and brought the glass to the boy's lips. "Swallow this, Lành. It'll make you better."

Feebly, the little boy gulped down the solution. Olio gently laid him back down on the blanket, and, slowly, the boy's eyes drooped closed again. When it was certain Lành was in a deep and sedated sleep, Etienne took out a small knife from his coat pocket. Adelene sat down by the deck of the cockpit with her knees in her chest, huddled fretfully against Lily. She squeezed her eyes shut.

34 OBLIVIOUS

Etienne was sitting with his knees close to his chest and his elbows on his knees. He was looking at Lánh, who lay asleep against Henry. The binding around the wound behind the little boy's ear was falling off, but Etienne did not reach out to place it back, because the cut had stopped bleeding. The little boy's face had gained back some of its color, and he slept soundly.

Adelene stood up and came to sit beside Etienne without a word, and for a while neither of them spoke. Then finally, when she had waited long enough and he had said nothing at all, "Are you alright?" she asked.

"Yes, I'm fine. I'm just tired," he answered.

"You should get some sleep. He'll be alright. You've done all you could for him today." She smiled. Her eyes tried to meet his but Etienne looked down at the floor between his knees, his eyes dark and pensive. "Thank you," she added, "for everything."

He shook his head. "No. Thank you. For making me realize how ignorant I'd been all these years."

"You weren't the only one, you know. If it weren't for my father, and Sara and Hacker, I would never have realized how trapped we were, how false and corrupt our world was. And if it weren't for you, none of us would be where we are now. You've got no reason to blame yourself. You're no different." Gently, she took the strange metal object from his hand and flipped it between her fingers, tilting her head and frowning slightly as she inspected it.

"How did you know he had this thing behind his ear?" She handed it back to him and he took it.

At first she thought he wouldn't answer. Then he took a deep breath, as if what he was about to say required all the air his lungs could hold. He sighed, and finally he said, "The same thing happened to my friend two years ago. It was right here." He pointed at a spot on his forearm and pressed his finger against it. "Under the skin."

She waited, but he said nothing more. Etienne looked out through the large cockpit window that opened onto the stars. He knew the *Inceptum Fidelis* was somewhere among those stars, far, far behind the little ship.

Adelene didn't go away. He wanted her to go away, but she didn't. She sat patiently next to him. Etienne looked down at the floor again. "There's no point in talking about it."

"Sometimes it helps to talk about things that stay buried inside us for too long," she said assuredly, sitting a bit closer to him. "Go on."

"It's a long story."

"I'll listen. I promise."

He didn't look up. When he began, it was in a low voice, almost a whisper. "Tobias was like a brother to me. We had been inseparable since Primary School, and some people even thought we were related. But we had our differences. I was much more daring than Tobias was. Much more rebellious and stubborn. Henry belonged to Tobias but everyone always thought the dog was mine. We were the adventurers; Tobias was the quiet kid who read books. I was the one who found the old barn in the Twenty-First. Once we found out that there were no microbots roaming around the place, we would go there everyday, and talk on and on about anything we wanted. It felt good to speak without worrying about whether the Authorities could hear us or not. Then one day I brought the banned books and hid them there. When I had read all of them I convinced Tobias to do the same. At first he was afraid to do so, but when he finally agreed he read them more avidly than I had. He was an intelligent guy, but until then he had never had the chance to develop that intelligence fully. It was like reading those books had set him free.

'Soon, he became more pensive, more talkative and rebellious. I saw this as a good thing until one day, about a year ago, he crossed a line. We were at my house, just the two of us and he started telling me he wished he could go back to Earth. He had seen it, he said, when he was barely a year old, before the Departure. He said that sometimes he remembered the Sun and the way it looked and felt, and how once you had seen it you never forgot it. I didn't believe him. 'Come on, Tobias, you were too young to remember,' I said, and laughed a little. But he didn't take it jokingly, and he said, 'Maybe I was, but I still have dreams about it."

"'Tobias, dreams like that—about going back to Earth— everyone has them but they're pointless. Irrational. Selfish.'

"'Selfish?' he said, 'So it's selfish to want a future? Did you choose to live on a ship your whole life, with no hope or ambition, knowing that you're the sacrificed generation? Our children will be heading towards a New World, but what are *we* heading towards? Nothing.'

"'We're part of this mission too, you know. Each and every one of us. What we're doing for humanity is honorable and you can't degrade it like this. Think of our parents. Do you think they had a choice? My parents were on the brink of extreme poverty. Your parents were illegal immigrants. We are safer here than we'd ever be if we had stayed on Earth."

"About as safe as a bunch of bottled-up flies, yes. Controlled by a dictator who takes away whatever freedom we have left.'

"'The Onweald keeps order. That's the way things are. You have to get used to the way things are.'

"Tobias walked to the living room window and crossed his arms and pressed his elbows against the windowsill. His eyes wandered across the fields and houses, and past the horses that grazed under the calm evening Lights, and then I thought I saw him look at the Great Wall that jutted from the earth a couple hundred meters from the house. You could distinguish it behind the trees, almost invisible, hiding itself. We all knew it locked us in but we ignored it. 'It's not how it should be,' Tobias said quietly. When I asked him what he meant he became impatient. 'Don't you understand that everything we're told is bullshit? All they're doing is brainwashing us so that we don't complain, so that They can continue to control us.'

"I started thinking he was out of his mind. 'Tobias, what are you saying?'

"'You know exactly what I'm saying. Why can't we speak our thoughts, our ideas, our dreams? Why are all those books we keep in the shack banned? Why do we have to wear these all the time?" He threw his glasses against the floor. 'I don't need glasses. I'm not nearsighted at all. Actually, I can see very far. Farther than any of you.'

"'What the hell is wrong with you?'

"'Look around, Etienne. You wear those glasses or contacts and you have all the information of the world in front of your eyes. But stare at an image of the Earth, and what information comes up? That it's an awful place to be. It's just another part of His plan. The Authorities are manipulating us."

"From the corner of my eye I could see Jexter walking towards us. He was listening. I was suddenly afraid. 'Tobias, just calm down.'

"'Don't tell me what to do!'

"I stepped back cautiously. Jexter was standing right behind me now, quietly. 'Tobias. Listen to me.'

"'No, you listen! The Onweald doesn't give a damn about us because he knows that as long as we fear him, he stays in power. But it doesn't have to be that way!'

"'Tobias, The Onweald is a good man! You're not making any sense!'

"Jexter stood next to me. His eyes were red as fire. 'The Onweald is all-seeing and all-powerful,' the robot said, 'All who speak against His Excellence are a nuisance to the colony and must be Detained.' He sounded as if he was reciting a verse from some kind of sacred pledge. Jexter had never seemed this threatening to me before. I wanted to run out of the room and keep on running until all of this was far behind me.

"'The Onweald is a weak, self-centered tyrant,' Tobias spat out, his eyes full of hatred. Jexter darted at him. I tried to stop Jexter. I tried to convince him that Tobias didn't mean what he said, but Tobias heard me, and he blurted out, 'I mean exactly what I say, and I say we turn this ship around!'

"In a flash Jexter had him immobilized with both hands behind his back. The android was mumbling to himself, sending some kind of signal to the Police, and Henry barked hysterically behind the door. I stood there with my feet frozen in the ground and I watched on, too afraid to be taken along with him. I watched on and said nothing.

"Before the Police droids dragged him out of the house, he looked into my eyes, and his eyes said, 'Do something, Etienne. Tell them it's not right. Tell them they can't do this.' But to me the horrible truth was that they could. The Authorities had the right to take Tobias away, because the Onweald was All-Powerful. I thought he had lost his mind, but the truth is I had lost mine.

"They told Tobias's family that he was well taken care of, that They were rehabilitating him from an apparent illness, and that he would be sent home once the process was over. I wanted to believe what They said, but I couldn't. It sounded strange. And yet everyone around me seemed to trust the Authorities unconditionally. Tobias Backlund was being cured from his illness, and there was nothing to worry about. The matter faded away. No one showed concern. No one questioned anything. No one said a word that could have been taken as an Offense towards Them, towards the Authorities under His orders. Everyone was scared, but we all hid it deep down in our minds behind a web of naive nonsense.

"A week passed. Soon I took Henry home with me. Tobias's family was glad to have one less of a thing to take care of in Tobias's absence. A month later, my father knocked at the door of my room and told me Tobias was finally back. I took my bike and rushed to his house. I found him lying motionless on the couch in the living room. His mother sat on a chair, watching over him quietly. As I approached I saw his eyes open slightly, and he looked at me. 'Tobias?' I said.

"He mumbled something but I couldn't hear what he said. I thought he was speaking to me and I moved closer. He spoke once more and this time I heard it. 'I should never have betrayed Him. I'm a traitor. His Excellency must forgive me. He is All-powerful, all-seeing... Feared and loved by all... For the good of Humanity, I shall follow him and he shall be the great Leader...' He spoke on and on in his somnolence, suddenly silent and then suddenly carried off into some kind of hallucination, as if hypnotized.

"'Is he alright?' I asked his mother.

"'He has been under a special treatment,' she answered, her voice imperturbably calm. There was a tinge of sadness in her eyes. 'They tried Their best to cure his illness, but he is not recovering well. We are very concerned about him. They say that coming home might help him. It reassures me to see that he has fallen asleep. He was in such a pitiable state when we took him in last night.'

"I stayed with them another hour. There was something terribly wrong with Tobias but I did not know what it was and no one would explain anything. I didn't know what to do. I didn't know what to say. I had no idea what to *think*. When I came back three days later, I found him in his room sitting up on his bed, staring blankly at the wall like a stone figure with no soul, but when he looked up at me I could tell he recognized me. "'Are you okay?' I asked.

"'I want to be alone,' he said. His voice was hoarse and frail. I tried to talk to him and say I was sorry, that I should have defended him when he was taken away, but he never answered, and so I left him alone. Then it came to me that maybe it would help him to see Henry again. The dog was at home with me and still hadn't seem his old master since the incident. It was below freezing outside the day I brought him with me to the Backlunds' house. Tobias's parents were surprised to see me stop by in such horrid weather, but they took me in warmly and asked me how I was.

"'I brought Henry,' I said.

"Tobias's father called Claire and Amber from the living room, and the two little girls rushed out of their rooms and embraced the big dog. He sat there panting happily with his tongue sticking out, and then he licked their faces and it made them grimace and giggle. Tobias's parents served me some tea and told me Tobias had gone for a walk outside.

"'In the cold?' I said, surprised.

"'Yes. He said he wanted to go out for a while,' his father said, 'He's gone out twice already and it did him good. He's much better now.'

"'He's more talkative,' his mother added, 'and he eats well.'

"I thanked them for the tea, said goodbye and walked back outside. The village was quiet, the lake was frozen and the small bridge down the road lay grayish under a sheet of sullen snow. Henry stayed close to me. I don't know how long we walked, the two of us, in the snow under the gloomy Ceiling hidden behind the clouds. We crossed the Outlet into the Twenty-First. We followed the pair of footsteps that led into the field across from which lay the shed. It could have been no one else that Tobias. I found him sitting down on a chair before the fireplace. He had come by himself, three kilometers from his house, and sat hunched over the fire with books in his hands. One by one, he threw them into the fire indifferently, like firewood.

"'Tobias! What are you doing?' I yelled. He wasn't throwing all of the books into the flames. Only the banned ones. I walked over to him and snatched them from his hands. He barely reacted. He stared at the flames licking the words off of the frail pages.

"'Give me those, Ettiene,' he said in a sort of monotone, his gaze plunged into the fire. He had bluish black circles under his eyes.

"'What are you doing?' I asked in a single exhale, despair choking my words.

"Tobias stood up and walked towards me, determined to take the books back. He stretched an arm out towards me. 'Give me the books,' he said, grinding his teeth in anger. I caught a glimpse of the metal syringe plunged under his skin. I saw that his hand was trembling.

"'What's wrong with you?'

"'Give me the books,' he repeated even louder.

"'No,' I shook my head, 'No. I won't give you anything, Tobias. You're sick. You have to go home.'

"'I'm not sick!' he started yelling. And he grabbed me by the shirt collar. 'Those books are banned! They must be burned! I'm not—I'm not *sick*!' The more I told him he had lost his mind, the more furious he got. He started saying I was an enemy of the Government, a traitor, an Askancist. He pinned me against the wall, took out a small knife and held it to my throat, making me drop the books. 'I'll kill you,' he hissed, 'I'll kill you.'

'Tobias! You're out of your mind, Tobias!' I tried to speak calmly, but I felt my heart pounding loudly in my chest. He held the knife to my throat and I felt the sharp coldness of the blade against my skin, and I thought he would kill me. I remember thinking it: *He's gonna kill me.*

He probably would've, if Henry hadn't been there with me. The dog, forgotten at my side, began to bark and growl threateningly at his old master. Tobias's attention was suddenly turned to Henry and he started wide-eyed into the dog's black pupils as if they held a glimmer of remembrance, a hint of the past that he had unconsciously forgotten. Slowly, he let go of me and lowered the knife, a pale look of shock anchored in his face. 'What's wrong with me?' he whimpered, his voice hoarse and tremulous. He dropped the knife and looked at his hands with stupor, as if he did not recognize them. "What's wrong with me?" Henry had brought back a piece of Tobias's lost soul, and Tobias caught a glimpse of himself in it, but he did not recognize the person he saw, and it tortured him.

"'Am I asleep?'

"I did not know what to answer. 'Yes,' I said, 'Yes, you are. And you need to wake up. Listen to me, Tobias. Try to wake up.'

"'I can't—' He passed his hands through his hair and

203

started pulling at it. 'I can't!' He was fighting against himself. He was fighting his madness. He was struggling to come back. And the worse is that he knew. 'They're killing me!' he cried out, 'They're killing me!' He knew he wasn't asleep, and somehow he knew what was happening, but he was helpless against it. I watched him storm out of the shack, I watched the cold and faceless wind envelope him, I watched him fade away behind the clouds of snow that filled the air, and I stood there stupidly, ignorantly. I watched him fall away.

I went out to look for him, and when I finally found him he was lying by the lake, dead. I sat by his body near the frozen water, in the snow, for hours. I remember rolling up his sleeve to look at that strange mechanism planted under his skin. And as I stared at it I knew that They had lied all along. What they had called a 'treatment' was not a treatment at all. It was a drug that had changed the way Tobias's mind worked. That's what it means to be Detained. They brainwash you, indoctrinate you, and inject that fluid in your bloodstream so that you become as robotic and senseless and They are and cause no more trouble. It's killing you without really killing you, but some people do die from it. The Authorities knew that Tobias was going to die, but they did not want to have anything to do with it, so They sent him home, and lied, and everyone found it best to believe Them."

Etienne plunged back into his thoughts. Adelene was still sitting beside him on the cold flooring, watching the tears in his eyes glisten in the light of the stars. The cockpit resounded faintly with the whir of the spaceship, loud enough to bring them back to reality. The others were still asleep.

"That's horrible," Adelene managed to say in a low, frail voice after a long pause. "I'm really sorry." She felt tears fill her own eyes as well. She thought of her father, gone for so many years, and of her mother... "Do you think—Do you think they could've done this to my parents as well?"

"I've heard that some people are able to resist the effects of the fluid. Those are the Detained who never come back."

"And what do They do with those people?"

"I don't know," Etienne said, "but we'll do whatever it takes to go back and save them. I promise you."

"But *how*?"

Etienne cast his dark eyes down at the metal object in his hands. He flipped it between his fingers. "We find a way to stop the Onweald."

35 ESTRANGED

It was dark. It was always dark. The resilient lights that illuminated the wide cockpit of the ship dimmed at a certain time and became brighter again at another, in cycles, simulating night and day, but after some time the many cycles felt blurred and mingled into greyness—neither night or day or anything at all. Maybe time passed and maybe it didn't. The ship glided on through space.

Adelene, Sylvan and Hacker sat close to one another against the cold white walls of the ship. "How long has it been since we left?" Adelene asked in a small voice.

"I'd say a month," Etienne said, taking a bite of out a cereal bar.

"I want to go home," Lành whined. "When are we going home, Adelene?"

"We're going to a new home, now, Lành. Earth is our new home, and it's a better home. We're going to get help there."

"Soon we'll go back and get Mommy?"

"Of course we will. And Daddy too."

Lành's tired eyes widened with curiosity. "But I thought Daddy was—"

"No, Daddy didn't pass away. The Authorities took him from us."

He gasped. "Why?"

"Because he stood up to Them, and They are weak. They don't like to be challenged. They are mean and can't be trusted. But don't worry, Lành, your Daddy is strong."

"Is he in a prison?"

"No, don't worry. The Authorities did not put him in a prison because they knew he was very strong and very intelligent." She held back her tears as well as she could. She held back the fear and sadness still encased inside her. She kissed Lành's forehead and smiled. "They take good care of him, but he wants to see us again. And we're going to get help."

"We'll go back and save him?" He held Henry's fluffy head on his knees and played with the dog's ears forgetfully.

"Yes. Once we find help, we'll go back and save him. I promise."

They didn't feel the ship slowing down, just as they had never felt it speeding up when it had taken off. Olio's ship was a strange ship. It moved through space without truly moving at all. It bended space-time, it manipulated energy. It made no sense to them and therefore they did not ask about it, nor even wonder about it. On the *Inceptum Fidelis*, they had all learned never to ask questions.

A calm robotic voice echoed across the ship. *Reaching end of calculated route*, it said, *Earth located at 340,000 kilometers from current location. Entering the atmosphere in: 26 minutes.*

Sara jumped to her feet and dashed to the great cockpit window. "We're here! We made it! Look! Look!"

The others gathered around the window, hooting and laughing as their eyes fell onto the vast blue orb, an asylum of life suspended calmly in the endless blackness of space. "We made it," Etienne said.

"I can see the clouds!" Lành squealed, pointing to the swirling white masses painted across the oceans and continents.

Entering Earth's atmosphere in: 9 minutes.

As the ship loomed closer and closer, the planet seemed to grow wider, clearer, until finally the sheer size of it stole all the air from their lungs and their eyes passed silently across its overwhelming immensity. Henry barked excitedly.

"Everyone strap themselves down!" Olio shouted, "The ship's about the land."

Entering the atmosphere. Oxygen: 20.946%, Nitrogen: 78.075%, Argon: 0.9341%, Carbon Dioxide: 0.031%. Approximately 1% water vapor. Attention, now closing the interface. A metallic frame slid like an eyelid over the window, shutting them in darkness. Adelene felt her heart pounding in her chest. She held Lành's hand and closed her eyes.

Mean Surface Temperature: 13 degrees Celsius. Surface pressure: 101.33 kilopascal. Equatorial surface gravity: 0.99732 g. Equatorial rotation velocity: 1,674.4 kilometers per hour...

The ship rumbled and roared and shook. It descended into the sky for what seemed an eternity. The small group confined inside waited in wordless apprehension. Then finally it began to decelerate. The rumbling faded away and the shaking stopped. The ship came to a stop with one last jolt.

Silence.

"I'm scared, Adelene," Lành whispered.

Sylvan sat crouched in a corner, clutching the jar with

the bumblebee. Lily hugged her knees into her chest. They waited. No one moved. No one spoke.

Silence.

United States of America, State of Michigan, the robotic voice hummed, *Six hours and thirty minutes Post Meridiem, local time. Elevation: 305 meters. Outside temperature, -6 degrees Celsius.*

With a solid, mechanical hiss, the broad entrance gate on the side of the ship slowly opened, and locked into the snow-covered earth with a firm clank. Henry yapped excitedly. Huddled together in the obscurity, they peered through the entrance with silent, alienated eyes. Outside, the wind howled. Waves of snow twirled in dense clouds, pallid and bitter. There was not a sound but the dismal wailing of the wind and the droning of the solitary spacecraft. The grey darkness and the cold swallowed the horizon.

There was no sign of life.

Slowly, hesitantly, Adelene walked to the entrance and stepped down the sloped rail, squinting at the falling snow. She took a deep breath, taking in the glacial air, then folded her arms over her chest and looked down at her feet. She stepped off the metal ramp and let her shoes sink into the powdery snow. Her worn shoelaces were still tied in the familiar double loop that the Cleaners always made. This, like everything else from the past, felt so far behind her now. The clouds of snow were too thick to reveal the Sky, but she knew that it was there, everywhere above her. "Where are we?" she whispered. The icy bite of winter left her cheeks rosy and cold.

"What if we're wrong?" Abebi's voice sounded behind her. The young girl stood in the doorway, her frizzy black hair dotted with snowflakes.

"What do you mean?" They felt the cold penetrate

through their clothes. It made them shiver and they rushed back into the ship.

"I mean… What if we're alone out there? What if they're all… gone."

"That's a stupid thing to say," Sara scoffed, "There's bound to be *someone* out there who can help us." The rigidity in the tone of her voice betrayed her apprehension.

"In any case, we'll have to wait a few hours to find out." Etienne made a leash out of a piece of rope and tied it around Henry's neck.

"He's right," Hacker said, standing in the entranceway and staring pensively at the icy greyness that stretched into the distance, "We have to wait until the weather clears up. We can't go out in the storm like this—Not without knowing where we're going."

Abebi coughed. Lily handed her a wool pullover.

Sylvan opened his jar and placed another sugar cube at the bottom. The bumblebee flew out just as he was about to close the lid again. Finally free, the little black dot of life found the entrance of the ship and obliviously hummed away into the blizzard.

"Is he going to be alright, Adelene?" Lành asked, huddled against his sister.

"Who?"

"Sylvan's bumblebee. He flew away into the cold…"

"Yes, he'll be alright."

"But it's so cold! I do hope he'll be alright. Why is it so cold outside?"

"Because there's a snowstorm."

"Why?"

"Because here there is nothing to control the weather, Lành. It does whatever it wants. It's free, just like the people who live here."

"And where *are* those people?"

"We have to go look for them."

"I want to go home."

"I know. I know." Adelene sighed. "I do too."

They closed the entrance and waited. They waited for hours. The storm persisted. After some time—it must have been well into the night—Etienne stood up and said, "I'm going out." He slipped his coat on and wrapped a scarf around his neck."

"Alone?" Adelene said.

"Out *there?*" Sara added, "You've got to be joking!"

"We can't keep on waiting like this. The storm's not dying out and we have to find help. All of you stay here and keep warm, I'll take Henry with me—Come on, boy!"

"Wait!" Olio came up to him and handed him a small metal device. "Take this. It's a tracker. I'll know where you are."

Etienne thanked him and was gone before any of them could call him back, Henry close by his side, wagging his tail and sniffing the cold snow-coated ground until the falling snow engulfed them both.

The others waited in silence. Abebi coughed again. Adelene frowned at the merciless gale weaving together snow and sleet. It concerned her to know that Etienne was out there in the cold, even with Olio's tracker. It was dark outside now, and the darkness strengthened the silence, the loneliness, the estrangement. Time passed excruciatingly slowly. The lights of the spacecraft had dimmed.

"You should get some sleep, Adelene." Sara lay huddled against the wall across from her, half of her face concealed in the shadows. "We'll be alright, you know. We have one another."

Adelene nodded detachedly. She looked around at the

others. Sylvan was so quiet it was hard to remember he was with them at all, but she could see him there, in the corner by himself. Lily had fallen asleep on Hacker's shoulder, and Lành was still nestled against Adelene, breathing evenly. He must have been asleep as well. Slowly her own eyelids sank over her eyes. She tried to open them again, but soon yielded to her exhaustion.

It was the barking in the distance that shook them all awake. "Do you hear that?" Lily said. They all sprung to their feet and opened the entrance.

They looked out into the night, ignoring the icy air that washed over them. Henry materialized from the snowy darkness and jumped into the ship, shaking the snow off his back.

"They're back!" Sara said gladly, "Etienne!"

Etienne's tall figure emerged through the snow. He held one arm over his eyes, shielding himself from the snow as he walked onto the ship. They took him inside and placed a blanket over his shoulders.

"Did you find anything?" Abebi asked impatiently.

"Let him catch his breath," Hacker said.

"I'm fine. I'm fine." Etienne panted. His hair stuck to the melted sleet on his face. "There's a house. Not far— Not far from here."

"A house?" Adelene exclaimed enthusiastically. "Was it occupied?"

"Yes, that's how I found it. I saw the light coming from one of the windows. And they have a barn. With horses."

"Why didn't you go knock?" Lily asked.

"I didn't want to frighten the habitants. This seems to be a very isolated area. People here are probably not used to disturbances in the middle of the night." He coughed hoarsely and leaned back against the wall. "I need some rest. I can't believe I found my way back here. It's all because of Henry. You're a good boy, Henry." The dog nuzzled his shaggy face against his master, panting happily. He was wet and shivering.

"We can send the kid," Hacker suggested, leaning against the wall and staring pensively down at the floor.

"Send Lành?" Adelene gasped.

"A kid can't scare them."

Sara stood up. "Hacker's right," she said, "They won't keep their door closed on a lost little boy in a snowstorm. Etienne can lead us to the house and we'll let Lành knock at the door. We'll stay out of sight."

"I don't want anything to happen to him, Sara," Adelene said faintheartedly.

Sara smiled gently. "Adelene, you're the little sister I never had. We trust each other, remember? It'll be all right. I promise."

After a long pause, Adelene gave an acquiescent nod and bent down to. "Put your coat on, Lành. We're going outside now."

The little boy rubbed his drowsy eyes with his hands. "But, Adelene, I'm tired."

"I know. So am I." She bent down to tuck the cashmere scarf around his neck into his buttoned coat. "Once we get to the little house Etienne told us about, the people living there will help us. It won't be long before we all get a good, warm bed to sleep in. Alright?" She kissed Lành on the cheek, and then she turned to Sara and hugged her. "Thank you," she said. Afterwards, she wondered why she had thanked her. Was it for reassuring her? For being there for her? Maybe it was just because Sara was the person who understood her, who protected her, who loved her. Sara would never leave her or her brother behind.

Adelene turned to Olio. "Stay with the ship. We'll come back to get you soon, O.K?"

The little robot nodded and took her hand. "Take care," he said.

From the spacecraft, with the blue lights of his eyes gleaming vigilantly in the blurry night, Olio watched the eight refugees walk away into the waves of snow, into the darkness, into the foreignness of it all. And then when they had disappeared from his sight, he sat down behind the entrance but did not close it. He gazed on into the blizzard for a long while, as if they would be safe from harm as long as he kept watch.

They had landed in a world of snow and darkness, foreign and unwelcoming. There were no Walls to set its limit. It went on and on in all directions, and the idea was disconcerting, dizzying, strange. They felt alone and insignificant. They held on to one another as if they had nothing else to hold onto. They walked on. Etienne carried Lành in his arms and Adelene walked next to him, never losing sight of him. Henry trailed along, stopping here and there to stick his large black muzzle into the foreign, snow-covered earth.

When the house finally came into view, the snowstorm had dissipated and the snow twirled more peacefully in the soundless wind. A faint glow emanated from one of the windows, illuminating a low wooden fence that stretched to the shadowy barn not far from the house. Etienne motioned the others to follow him and the group staggered up to the barn and crouched down behind it, panting out clouds of vapor into the frozen wind. They looked up at the wooden wall and touched it with their hands. The robust firmness of it reassured them. All else was grey haze, confusion and shadows.

Lành bent down and took something in his hands—a frail black form stirring feebly in the snow. He stared down at it, studied it, and talked to it softly. Then, he sheltering it in his cupped hands and cowered next to Sara and Adelene. "I'm cold," he muttered.

The others were too preoccupied to hear him. "They have horses in here," Etienne said, "I heard them neighing. If anything, we could ask the habitants for a horse, and directions to the nearest town."

It took some time for them to convince Lành that they were not abandoning him, and that they would stay right here, but after hugging his sister once last time the boy finally agreed to walk up to the door alone. Henry tried to follow him, but Etienne tugged at the dog's leach and held him back. Lành stumbled cautiously across the snowy property, bundled up in warm layers of clothing. The wind had molded a thin coat of ice in inky smears along the surface of the snow, which rose almost to his knees. He made his way hesitantly to the doorstep, and they watched him ring the doorbell. He looked back at the darkness to catch sight of Adelene.

"I'm still here, Lành," she whispered, knowing he couldn't hear her.

Through the falling snow, they saw the door open and warm light pour out onto the little boy. An old woman stood in the doorway, clutching her shawl against her chest. Lành had never seen an old woman before, but Adelene couldn't tell whether he was afraid or not. He said something to her, and she seemed to answer, but from the shadows of the barn it was impossible to catch any of the words. By the woman's side stood a tall Familiar, but it held almost no resemblance to those on the *Inceptum Fidelis*. The android's body looked smoother and less jagged in design. It's eyes were red, but it was a warm red, peaceful and welcoming compared to the icy sapphire of Myrna's eyes. This Familiar did not give orders. It did not seem in charge. It was the woman who had opened the door.

Lành stepped across the threshold of the doorway and disappeared inside the little house. Adelene held her breath. The wind howled. Time crept painfully on. "Do you think he's okay?"

Then the door opened again and Lành's little face appeared, shadowy against the light from inside. "Adelene!" he called out into the night, "Adelene, come!" The little boy took a few steps forward and searched the darkness with his eyes.

The woman walked out into the snow and called out as well, "Don't stay out in the cold like this, children, come!" The woman's voice was frail, and difficult to hear above the wind, but it was full of gentle kindness and humanity. Adelene wondered if this was how grandmothers were— caring, gentle and welcoming. The girl brushed the snowflakes from her eyelashes, and, still dissimulated in the blue-black shadows, she smiled. She motioned the others to follow as she stepped forward.

"All of you, come in! You poor dears!" The woman watched the six of them materialize into the light of her home, her face washed with concern and perplexity. They looked up at her cautiously and gave a slight bow of the head, one after the other, bundled in their layers of rich clothing.

"Thank you, *Domina*," Sara said politely, "You are very kind."

The woman made a gesture with her hand. "Please, come inside where it is warm. Goodness! You poor, poor things!"

The snowfall had died down. Just before she passed across the threshold of the door, Abebi tapped Adelene's shoulder and pointed to the Sky. It was a white crescent of light floating quietly between the clouds of the passing storm. *The Moon,* Adelene thought. There was a smile on her lips and in her eyes, and the smile flew gently into her heart. She looked up at the Moon and knew that all the stars were there with it, and that this time there was no Ceiling to ever lock them out.

I'll come back, Adelene whispered to the stars. *I'll do whatever I can to save you. I promise.* A tear of sadness and joy fell from her eyes.

She closed the door gently behind her.

ABOUT THE AUTHOR

Juliette Rogasik is a young French author who writes exclusively in English. She was born in Paris, and grew up traveling consistently between Europe and the United States. She is currently studying Comparative Literature with Film Studies at King's College, London. After having spent eight months in an American suburban town in her third year of high school, at 17, she decided to write *The Walls of Flemington*, a novel that somehow brings up the superficiality of suburbia's carefully manicured perfection. Underneath, a homogenous consumer society walled in on itself, trapped in the monotonous boredom of conventionality. She was also very inspired by Richard Adam's *Watership Down*, a powerful fable on humanity— its vulnerability, fear of the unknown, constant search for "home"— and its struggle between the comfort of uniformity and the uncertainty of change. Today, Juliette lives between New York and London.

Printed in Great Britain
by Amazon.co.uk, Ltd.,
Marston Gate.